Killer's Range

Killer's Range

WAYNE C. LEE

Sagebrush
Large Print Westerns

Library of Congress Cataloging in Publication Data

Lee, Wayne C.
   Killer's range / Wayne C. Lee.
      p.   cm.
   ISBN 1-57490-237-7 (hc : alk. paper)
   1. Western stories. 2. Large type books. I. Title
   [PS3523.E34457W56   1996]
   813'.54--dc20   96-42252
                                                                  CIP

Cataloguing in Publication Data is available from
the British Library and the National Library of Australia.

Sagebrush Large Print Westerns are published in the
United States and Canada by Thomas T. Beeler, Publisher,
Box 659, Hampton Falls, New Hampshire 03844-0659.
ISBN 1-57490-237-7

Published in the United Kingdom, Eire, and the Republic of
South Africa by Isis Publishing Ltd, 7 Centremead, Osney
Mead, Oxford OX2 0ES England. ISBN 0-7531-6133 8

Published in Australia and New Zealand by Australian
Large Print Audio & Video Pty Ltd, 17 Mohr Street,
Tullamarine, Victoria, 3043, Australia. ISBN 1-86340-358-7

Manufactured in the United States of America by Sheridan
Books in Chelsea, Michigan.

CHAPTER 1

IT TAKES SOME MEN THIRTY YEARS TO REACH SUCH A degree of maturity that they are ready to meet the test of life and prove their worth. Some reach it in twenty-five; a few in even shorter time. It all depends on the steel that is in a man and the way that steel has been tempered.

At twenty-two, Troy Willouby was ready to meet the test. Tall and lean and hard, he sat the saddle of his blue roan as if both saddle and rider were a part of the horse. His gray eyes swept the wide valley below him, picking out familiar landmarks. He was, ready for the test and he knew it. But his brother, Boone, on the black beside him, was not ready. That he also knew.

Troy pulled his eyes away from the valley and looked at his brother. The sun had not burned Boone's fair skin as deeply as it had Troy's, nor did the soft blue eyes reflect the hardness and bitterness that Troy knew were in his own. Boone Willouby would be as out of place here as Troy would have been behind a desk in Denver.

"You can pull out now, Boone," Troy said, reading his brother's thoughts as Boone swung his eyes over the valley. "I won't hold it against you."

"Dad would."

"I'll take care of Dad. You're not cut out for what's ahead."

"I know that. But I'm a Willouby."

"That won't be enough. That gun don't fit your hand right."

Disgust tugged fleetingly at the corners of Boone's mouth. "A gun fits your hand like it grew there."

1

"I've trained it that way," Troy said softly, fingers touching the butt of the black-handled .45 at his hip.

"What good will it do you to kill, kill, kill?" Boone's fingers gripped his saddle horn, the knuckles white. "That won't bring Mother or Ralph or Susie back to life."

"We're not coming back just for revenge," Troy said, his voice low and granite-hard, "although there are a lot of snakes down there that need stomping. We had a fine ranch here once, and we got run off. I figure we'll take that back."

"Not without fighting."

"I hope there is a fight," Troy breathed, his eyes roving the valley like a stalking cougar.

"Dad's not interested in the ranch," Boone said after a pause. "He's coming back for revenge, nothing else."

"He's got a right to. If either one of us had had a wife and two youngsters killed in cold blood right in our own house, I reckon we'd be after revenge, too."

"It won't do any good. And the killing won't all be on one side."

"Maybe not." Troy raised his eyes to Boone's soft-skinned face. "So you'd better deal yourself out of this while you can."

Boone shook his head. "The Willoubys have always stuck together. They'll stick together now. If it wasn't for Dad we wouldn't be riding into this. For eight years he's harped on nothing but coming back here and evening the score."

"Dad tucked his tail and ran once. That's been eating on him like a cancer ever since. I know about how he feels. He's got to come back and make his stand or he'll never feel like a man again."

"You're like him that way, aren't you, Troy? You

could never show yellow and hold your head up again."

"I don't figure on trying it."

Boone pulled out a small pocket watch. "Must be about time for the stage. Where do you aim to stop it?"

Troy jerked a thumb towards the lower end of the valley, where the stage road wound out of the hills and headed up Storm Creek before angling up a tributary to Big Pine. "We'll catch it down there just before it comes out in the open."

Boone nodded, then pointed down the notch cut by Storm Creek in its escape from the valley. "There it comes now. Why didn't we meet it farther back in the hills? We'll be inviting trouble this close to town."

"That notch is better than five miles from town. We can get Dad and lose ourselves back in these hills before the stage can get to town. That notch is the only place along the road where we won't leave tracks."

"Tracks!" There was cutting bitterness in Boone's voice. "You'd think we were outlaws the way we have to sneak around."

"The Willoubys didn't have a friend in the valley when we left here eight years ago. There's no reason to think there are any now."

"We'd better go," Boone said nervously.

Troy nodded, switching his gaze from the valley to the road where the stage was laboring up a grade. No hurry yet, and he waited, searching the area around the mouth of the notch.

"What are we waiting for now?" Boone demanded impatiently. "Why did we come up here in the first place? We could have gone directly to the stage road."

Again Troy nodded. "It might just be possible that it leaked out we were coming. That would call for a reception party. This is the best place to spot it."

3

"Not much chance of that."

Troy looked through narrowed lids at his brother. "There is some chance, though, Boone. And that's something we can't take."

They reined into a trail leading down towards the valley, and Troy moved into the lead, Boone falling naturally behind. Troy led a saddled horse and Boone had a pack animal in tow. Pines closed about them, their scent heavy in the still morning air. A woodpecker hammered vigorously on a dead tree, and a jay scolded them as they passed.

Then they were out of the trees, almost on a level with the notch.

At that moment they came—four riders—and even at that distance Troy could see they were masked. They came from the rocks to the north of the road and formed a barrier across the path of the stage.

The big Concord coach swayed through the notch and rocked to a halt as the driver leaned back on the reins and set the brakes.

"What do you make of it?" Boone asked, reining up.

"Somebody found out we were coming." Troy spurred his horse, pulling the lead animal at arm's length down the slope towards the notch.

A sense of disaster gripped Troy, almost choking the breath from him. Death blocked the stage road down there at the notch. The first blow in the Willoubys' fight for the home they had been forced to leave was about to be struck. And the Willoubys wouldn't do the striking.

Under the threat of steady guns, two passengers climbed down from the coach. Troy recognized the big square-built frame of Dan Willouby.

He wasn't close enough to see all that was happening, but he could read sign. The time was right for Dan

4

Willouby to make a desperate back-to-the-wall fight. Then Troy realized with sinking despair that the guns Dan was to wear were still in the pack on the horse Boone was leading.

It wasn't a fight, for Dan had nothing with which to fight. Troy heard the roar of a gun and saw Dan go down.

Blind rage born of his helplessness tore at Troy. His gun was in his hand and he was prodding his horse savagely. But the raiders saw him and wheeled back into the rocks, spurring away before Troy could do more than fire some futile shots after them.

At the stage, he pulled up and dismounted, fighting down the burning urge to ride after the killers and make them face his blazing guns. The stage driver still sat glued to his seat as if unable to do more than hold the lines on his nervous horses. The second passenger, a middle-aged woman, was leaning weakly against the rear wheel, her face as colorless as a sun-bleached dish towel.

Troy barely gave them a glance as he dropped on his knees beside his father. With steady fingers he felt for pulse beats. Only when Boone rode up and slid off his horse did he look up.

Boone's face was a mask of shock and horror. "Dead?" His voice was only a croak.

Troy shook his head. "He's hit bad, but he's got a chance." He stood up, his eyes settling coldly on the flabby woman still cowering against the wheel. "Who was it, lady?"

She shook her head, then opened her mouth, but no sound came. The driver finally shifted on his seat. "Ain't no way of telling who it was," he said. "They was all masked."

5

"It was somebody who lived here," Troy said, his eyes boring into the driver. "You know everybody in this valley, don't you?"

"I reckon I do. But I ain't saying I ever seen these critters before."

Troy switched back to the woman. "Get in. You're moving on."

The woman moved with startling swiftness for her size, stepping gingerly past Dan and up into the coach. "Go on," Troy told the driver.

The driver didn't move. "Ain't you going to load him on?" He jerked his head towards Dan. "There's a doc in Big Pine."

Troy's hand fisted. "I said, go on!"

"Want me to send out the doc?" the driver insisted.

"We'll get a doc if he's needed."

"But he might have a chance if Doc Holmes could work on him."

Troy's hand dropped to his gun. "I told you to travel." His gray eyes burned steadily into the driver.

The man fidgeted with the lines and turned away from Troy's stare. "Sure, sure. You ain't no better than the other killers." He slapped the lines, and the coach lurched up the road towards Big Pine.

"Why did you send him on?" Boone asked in a hushed tone as the stage faded into a curtain of dust. "Is Dad beyond the help of a doc?"

Troy turned to the extra horses. "No."

"Then why, if there's a doctor in town?"

"The only kind of medicine he'd get in Big Pine would be another dose of lead poisoning. If they'd take a chance on holding up a stage to get a shot at the Willoubys, you can imagine what they'd do if there was a Willouby in town flat on his back."

6

Boone slid from his saddle hut clung to the horn as if his knees wouldn't hold him. "Doesn't Dad need a doc?"

Troy led the extra saddle horse up beside Dan. "He's got to have one. But we'll bring the doc. It may be too late by the time we get him, but it would have been sure death to have sent Dad to town. Give me a hand here."

Quickly Troy bound up Dan's wound so that the flow of blood was checked.

Carefully they lifted Dan into the saddle and tied him so he couldn't fall.

"Where to now?" Boone asked then.

"The cave where we've been planning to go. And we'd better be moving. We can't travel very fast with Dad."

"You think we might be followed?"

"Maybe. When the stage gets in, they'll find out they didn't finish their job. They're apt to come back to tend to that."

About noon, they topped a heavily timbered ridge, and Troy caught the sound of a stream tumbling over the rocks below. A virgin stand of ponderosa pine matted the canyon, and an occasional blue spruce broke the dark green monotony. The air was still, and warmer than usual for this early in the spring. The threat of a thunderstorm hung in the white-capped thunderheads in the west.

The horses dropped down the slope and splashed across the stream. There Troy turned them upstream along the bank, where there appeared a flat grassy bench as though it might once have been a trail.

Troy watched Dan anxiously as the miles slipped behind, feeling for his pulse from time to time. It remained weak but steady, although Dan showed no

7

sign of regaining consciousness. And always Troy kept an eye cocked on the back trail. He met Boone's worried eyes.

"You don't think they can follow the trail we've left, do you?" Boone asked.

"I hope not," Troy said. "But any chance is too big for us to take. Even if we're careful, we can't always win." He nodded towards Dan as proof.

Troy left the creek and reined up a side canyon that reached like an arm back towards the main valley. In places fallen trees, monarchs of an age now past, sent them on short detours. Then, where the sides of the canyon fell back in a long slope, Troy left the canyon floor and headed up the slope, following a ledge that sliced up the mountainside as far as the eye could follow it through the trees.

Near the top, Troy reined up before the mouth of a cave that was hidden from the valley by trees. Two huge pines stood at the mouth of the cave.

"We'll make Dad as comfortable as possible," Troy said, dismounting. "Then I'll go for a doctor while you do what you can for Dad and keep an eye on the valley from the look-out."

Boone looked over the place carefully. "It hasn't changed much since we used to play here," he said softly. "But I never thought we'd have to live here."

Carefully, they lifted Dan off the horse and carried him inside the cave. It was dry and cool there; the dust was like powder and an inch deep. Dan stirred as they laid him down and placed a bedroll under his head. His eyes opened, and Troy could see by the light coming from the cave entrance that fever had set in.

"You're all right, Dad," he said quietly. "I'm going to bring a doc to check you over."

Dan stared around for a minute; then his eyes fastened on Troy. "It was Slagg, Troy," he muttered thickly. "I recognized him. He's the first one to get."

The effort was too much for Dan, and he sank back, his eyes closing. Troy gave thought to Dan's words. He remembered Cy Slagg, a horse rancher out north-east of Big Pine close to the Jericho Hills, a big coarse man whom the boy had never liked. Troy looked up and caught Boone's eyes on him. The color had left Boone's face and his fists were knotted at his sides.

"You're not going after Slagg, are you?"

Troy shook his head. "Not now. I'm going after the doc in Big Pine. Slagg can wait."

Troy walked to the cave mouth and waited for Boone to follow. "Take the packs inside and get some dry wood for a fire," he said. "Be sure the wood is dry. We don't want smoke giving us away. Make Dad as comfortable as you can; then go up the ledge to the look-out and see what's going on in the valley. I'm going to use the Deer Creek trail, so if anybody should see me leaving the main valley he won't guess where we're hiding out. Be at the look-out in a couple of hours when I bring the doc back. Make sure nobody follows us."

Boone nodded. "Better hurry with the doc," he said.

"I'll be back as quick as I can make it." Troy reached for the reins of his horse. "Be sure nobody follows me from town."

CHAPTER 2

As Troy and Doc Holmes neared the ranch on Storm Creek, a rider turned out of the yard and came

9

towards them. Troy shifted to the left side of the trail where his gun hand was unhampered.

"Don't get itchy-fingered," Holmes said, disgust in his voice. "That's only Mary."

Troy had already discovered the rider was sitting sidesaddle. His hand relaxed. "Who's Mary?"

"Mary Barstow. She lives at the ranch."

A body blow wouldn't have jarred him more. Barstow! And on the ranch the Willoubys once owned! But he should have known. Barstow was the ringleader of the murderers who had forced them out of the valley. Why wouldn't he take over the ranch?

He remembered Mary Barstow. She had been a gangling kid of ten the last time he'd seen her, with long braids the color of a sunflower petal. He had liked her then as much as a boy of fourteen could like a girl of ten. But that had been before the raid. He had scarcely thought of her since.

The girl slowed her horse as if half afraid as she approached the two riders. Then, apparently recognizing Holmes, she came on. Troy got a look at her then and could barely believe his eyes. Surely this wasn't the girl with the sunflower braids. She was of medium height and slender, and the freckles he remembered on her face were gone. Her hair, peeping out from under a wide-brimmed hat, was the color of spun gold, and Troy guessed it would be as soft as velvet to the touch. But it was her eyes that struck him most and held him like a magnet. They were blue, the color of the sky on a windless evening after the sun's last rays have faded and the purple shades of night have begun to creep in.

He tore his eyes away and suddenly remembered his manners enough to tip his hat.

"Hello, Mary," the doctor greeted her. "Everybody

10

well at your place?"

She smiled then, showing a row of even teeth. "We're fine, thank you, Doctor."

Holmes hesitated a second as if on the verge of saying something more. Then he nudged his horse forward.

"See you later, Mary," he called back.

They crossed the creek in silence; then Holmes said, "You knew Mary, didn't you?"

Troy nodded. "I went to school with her eight years ago. I doubt if I'd have recognized her, though, and I don't think she knew me."

"She didn't," the doctor said thoughtfully.

Holmes dropped into silence again, and Troy kicked his mount into a lope. When they slowed to blow the horses Troy asked a question.

"Does Mike Barstow control the whole valley?"

Surprise stamped itself on the doctor's face. "Barstow? From what I hear, he does well to control his own house."

Troy frowned. "That's not how I figured it. There should be a dozen ranches in this valley. Why aren't they here?"

"I've wondered that, too."

"Somebody bosses everything in this valley. He says who can have a ranch here and who can't. If it isn't Barstow, who is it?"

"I hadn't thought much about there being a boss. I've only been here six months."

"That ought to be long enough to find out who's the big finger."

The doctor frowned thoughtfully. "If there is a big boss here, I couldn't tell you who he is. He's never bothered me. It might be Barstow, but I doubt it."

"Who else could it be?" Troy pressed.

"If I were naming the most prominent men in and around Big Pine," Holmes said after a minute's thought, "I'd start with King Purdy. He owns the King's Palace and, I would guess, has more money than anybody in the valley. And here, like in any other place, money has a mighty loud voice. Then there's his right-hand man, Ace Belling. Belling is a dealer in the Palace. But neither of them have any interest in the ranches except to get the ranchers' money. Of course there's Slagg and Finley, two horse ranchers out east of town. And Eli Emitt, the sheriff. Sel Abitz runs the grocery store. But the only big thing about Abitz is his wife. I just don't see any range boss among them."

They reached the big rock under the look-out, and Troy pulled to a halt. Holmes followed suit, looking curiously around him.

"Is your father close?" he asked.

"Quite a way from here," Troy said.

"Then why are we stopping here?" Holmes asked impatiently.

"I'm afraid I'll have to put blinders on you now, Doc," Troy said.

Suspicion and anger clouded the doctor's face. "Blindfold me? There's no sense in doing that. I won't tell where I've been."

"I don't think you would, Doc. But in my position, I can't afford to take the chance."

Still the doctor hesitated, hands stacked on the saddle horn. "All right," he said finally. "I don't seem to have much choice. I might do the same if our positions were switched."

"Thanks, Doc." Troy moved over to tie on the blindfold. "I'm glad you didn't decide to be stubborn."

12

Taking the reins of the doctor's horse, he started along the foot of the front wall of Storm Range, finally turning into the blind canyon where he had come out into the valley earlier.

A half-hour later he led the doctor's horse up the slope to the mouth of the cave. There he stopped and dismounted as Boone came down the ledge from the look-out.

"Nobody followed you," Boone announced. "Better get the doc in there. Dad's been out of his head part of the time."

Troy helped Holmes dismount, leaving the blindfold in place. Only when he had led him inside the cave did he take the cloth off. The doctor blinked in the half-light of the cave, looking around him.

"Hiding out in a cave, are you?" he said. "I'll have to have more light than this or I can't examine anybody."

"We'll get you some light," Troy said. "And just forget you're in a cave."

Holmes smiled. "I don't know how I'm going to forget it now. But I won't remember when I get back in town. I promise that."

Troy went to one of the packs and dug out a big candle. He lighted it and carried it back to the doctor.

Holmes crossed to Dan. "Hold the light close," he said, and bent to his task.

It was a long session. Holmes called for hot water and more light. Boone carried in dry wood and made the fire roar while Troy brought out another candle and a holder and waited on the doctor as he worked.

"Is he very bad?" Troy asked once as the doctor paused to reach in his bag for another instrument.

"Bad enough." Holmes bent back to his task. "He's tougher than a pine knot or he wouldn't be alive now.

13

You put a good bandage on him, but he lost a lot of blood, anyway. It's a clean wound, going all the way through, but it came mighty close to some vital spots."

Finally the doctor pressed a clean bandage in place and stood up, wiping a hand over his forehead.

"What are his chances?" Troy asked bluntly.

"I wouldn't give two whoops in a dark night for the chances of an ordinary man in his condition. But he seems to be made of pretty tough fiber. He may make it. But if he does, it's going to be a long hard pull. Don't expect him up and around for a long time."

"We can't move him?"

Holmes shook his head. "You've moved him enough already. Move him again and it might as well be towards the cemetery."

Boone, listening, clenched his fists, despair washing over his face. "Then we'll have to stay here?"

Holmes looked at the younger Willouby. "I can't say about you." He jerked a thumb towards Dan. "But he'll stay awhile. He'll be dead if you try to move him."

"He won't be moved," Troy promised.

Holmes took some pills from his bag. "Give him one of these pills whenever he's in too much misery. Better not get too far away from him. I ought to look at him again in a couple of days."

"I'll come after you then," Troy said.

"I can meet you at the big rock," Holmes said. "I know the way that far."

Troy nodded. "Might be best. The fewer times I show up in town, the better off I'll be, I reckon."

Troy flipped out the blindfold and tied it on the doctor.

Boone followed them to the horses. "You're not going after Slagg, are you?" he asked, his voice low and

14

tense.

Troy helped Holmes mount, then turned to his brother. "I'm going to look for him."

"But killing him won't do any good."

"What do you expect me to do? Give him a medal?"

"You don't have to do anything."

Troy reached for the reins of his blue roan. "Slagg thinks he killed Dad. If we ever intend to show our faces in the valley, we've got to do something about Slagg."

Boone's face was twisted, and there was a sob in his voice as he almost screamed, "Go ahead! Kill! Kill! That's what you were born to do!"

Troy mounted and, leading the doctor's horse, started down the trail.

CHAPTER 3

AT THE ROCK, TROY UNTIED THE DOCTOR'S blindfold. "I'm sorry I had to do that, Doc."

Holmes rubbed his eyes. "No sorrier than I am. I can't say that I appreciate a ride over trails like that when I can't see where I'm going."

Troy dug a double eagle out of his pocket and handed it to the doctor. "Does that pay the bill?"

"More than pays it," Holmes said as he pocketed the gold coin. "This will cover the next visit, too. And it might pay for more than that if you forget the blindfold."

"I'll forget it as soon as I'm sure of you, Doc. You'll come here day after tomorrow? What time?"

"In the morning. About ten."

"I'll be here," Troy promised.

The sun had just touched the tip of the jagged peak

when Troy splashed across Storm Creek by the Barstow ranch. Almost involuntarily he pulled to a halt, his eyes swinging up the hill to the north of the house where three graves had been made eight years ago. The next minute he was guiding the roan towards the hill top.

Two rows of cottonwoods formed a barrier between the house and the hill. The hill itself was dotted with pines, as was every high spot in the valley. Scattered scrub pines grew all the way down to the cottonwoods by the house.

At the first of two large pines at the top of the hill, Troy dismounted and tied his horse. Between the two trees were three freshly tended graves. A perplexed frown wrinkled his brow. He hadn't expected to find any sign of the graves. Eight untended years would have wiped away all evidence of their existence. But the mounds had been carefully built up and kept free of weeds. Troy tried to think of anyone in the valley who might have shown that much consideration for a Willouby and found no answer.

Behind him a twig snapped, and he wheeled, his hand bringing up his gun. The slope seemed devoid of life. Then he caught a movement a few yards below him in the scrub pines. He waited, fingers tense on the gun.

Then he relaxed, quietly slipping the gun back in his holster. Mary Barstow was coming up the hill, apparently unaware of his presence. Golden head bent, eyes on the ground at her feet, she threaded her way through the trees up the dim path until she was within ten feet of Troy. There she looked up and stopped with a gasp, her hand flying to her mouth. But no sound came.

"Sorry I'm such a scary sight," Troy said.

She caught her breath. "I didn't expect to find anyone here. I never have before."

16

"You come here often?"

She nodded, then took her eyes away from him and looked out over the valley. "Lots of times. It's nice and quiet here."

"It is nice," he said. He looked out across the valley towards Big Pine on Pine Creek a mile away, then swung around to look at the ranch house just below. "Kinda makes you feel like you've crawled up above everything here."

She looked at him intently, a little frown puckering her forehead. "You're Troy Willouby," she said at last, recognition flooding over her. Then fear stamped itself on her face. "Why did you come back?"

The relaxed lines in Troy's face hardened as he turned to look over the graves. "I promised I'd be back."

"But why? You'll only cause trouble for yourself and everybody else." There was a catch in her voice.

He turned to her. "I wasn't looking for a bed of roses when I came back. I'm expecting trouble for myself and I'm aiming to make plenty for some other people. Somebody's got a lot of stuff belonging to the Willoubys. They didn't buy it, and I figure it's time they gave it back. Then there's another score to settle." He jerked a thumb towards the graves. "Who's been taking care of these?"

"I have," Mary said simply.

"Why?"

"They were neglected. There wasn't anyone else to take care of them. Then I'd heard stories of what happened to your mother and sister and brother."

"And you felt sorry for them?" Bitterness edged his words.

Mary shook her head. "Not for them. For you who were left. I saw you the day you left the valley, Troy.

17

You were full of hate then, hate for everybody here. I doubted if you'd ever get over it. That's why I felt sorry for you."

"You wouldn't expect the Willoubys to come back full of love and kisses for the people here, would you?" he asked.

"I was hoping you wouldn't come back at all."

He turned to her again. "After what they did to Mother and Susan and Ralph, do you think I could live with myself and not try to square things for them?"

She walked to one of the big trees and leaned against it. "I think I understand a little how you feel, Troy. But I've heard only one side of the story. Tell me your side."

"You wouldn't want to hear it."

She kept her eyes out over the valley. "I'll listen."

"We were the first family in this valley," Troy began, letting his memory reach far back. "Dad had worked in a bank back in Pennsylvania when he decided we should come west. We picked this spot right here and built that log house. I was eleven when we came. People followed us here in streams. The next year there were a half-dozen ranches in the valley, and the town of Big Pine was started. The third year more came, and they built a school in Big Pine. Your folks came that summer, and you started to school with the rest of us."

She nodded. "I remember. We came from Ohio. Dad took a homestead in eastern Nebraska. It wasn't a good place, quite a way from any neighbors. Then one night we had visitors, three strange men. They stayed all night. The next day Dad said we were moving on to a better place the men had told him about. We came here."

Troy fixed his eyes on the river below. "You came in

18

the summer and our trouble started in the fall. At first Dad was just told to move on. He didn't pay any attention. The warning was repeated several times, and each time it sounded more like a threat. Dad got worried, but he's stubborn. He wouldn't move. One man was making those threats. He said the valley wasn't big enough for him and the Willoubys." He looked at the girl. "That man was Mike Barstow."

She had been looking out over the valley as he spoke. She whirled towards him, the color draining from her face. "You're wrong, Troy. It couldn't have been."

He shook his head, tight-lipped. "I'm not wrong. Mike braced Dad whenever he saw him, and he got nastier each time. He never gave a reason for trying to run us out; just said the valley wasn't big enough for all of us. That went on all winter, but we boys in school didn't pay much attention because Dad didn't say much to us about it."

The color was creeping back into Mary's face. "Somebody made a mistake, Troy. Dad never said anything about trouble with the Willoubys. If he'd had trouble, he'd have told us."

Troy didn't look at the girl. "There was trouble, all right. I got a first-hand look just after school was out. It was the day of the raid. I was in town with Dad. Mike met us and warned Dad that he'd better leave the valley in three days if he didn't want something to happen to his family. I remember Dad was so mad he'd have killed Mike right there if he'd had his gun, but he'd left it in the wagon for some reason. Mike was about as nasty about it as he could be. I got mad that day, the first time I'd ever been mad at a grown man. Dad wouldn't have left the valley then without a fight, and I was ready to side him.

19

"We went home and told Mother and the rest of the kids. We didn't expect trouble for three days, at least, but Dad planned the way we'd fight off any attack that might come. He and Boone and I were to take the two windows and the door in the main part of the house, and Mother and Ralph and Susan were to stay in the bedroom where there wasn't likely to be any stray bullets. Mother could handle a rifle from there if she had to.

"They struck that night about eleven o'clock. We were caught by surprise, but we grabbed our rifles and ran to our posts in our nightshirts. It was bright moonlight, and we could see there were seven riders out front. They yelled that they were giving us our last chance to get out. Dad took a shot at them instead of answering.

"They piled off their horses, and scattered. They had plenty of ammunition and they weren't stingy with it. We couldn't see well enough to tell who the men were, but we had a good idea. They started creeping up on us, but they found that wasn't healthy. We could all handle rifles pretty well. We killed one of the raiders and hit another one. At least we found bloodstains on the grass later. The dead man was Hal Swazey.

"We expected them to rush us, but they only tried that once. That was the time we got Swazey. They backed off, and right after that got on their horses and left. Dad went into the bedroom to tell Mother and the kids they were gone. I'll never forget the look on his face when he came out.

"I couldn't believe it at first. There wasn't any reason for killing them. One or two of the raiders must have slipped around the house and gone through the window while the others were keeping us busy. The room was torn up some, but there was nothing there for them to steal. The next day we buried Mother and the kids here, and then we left. But I resolved I'd come back. And I have."

Troy finished his story, the words dying in the silence. He stood gazing down the valley, lost in bitter memories. He had forgotten Mary, and when she spoke, her voice: startled him.

"You've come back to get revenge on the men who made that raid?"

Troy didn't look around. "There was no law here then to punish them and there's no law now that will do it. The only kind of law men like that will respect is the kind I carry here." He tapped his gun.

"Do you know the men who were on that raid?" she asked in a low, frightened voice.

"Not all of them," Troy admitted. "There were seven. I reckon I can name four, Hal Swazey was killed there. And if Hal was there, it's a cinch Ed Swazey was, too. Hal and Ed were never far apart. And Cy Slagg must have been one of the gang. Else why would he have met the stage today and tried to kill Dad? And I don't reckon there's any doubt who the leader was. He'd threatened Dad all winter."

Mary came away from the tree where she had been leaning. "Not Dad!" she cried, fear draining the color from her face. "He wouldn't go on a raid like that. I know he wouldn't."

The face Troy turned to her was granite-hard and expressionless. "He made threats that something would happen to our family if we didn't leave. Was your dad home the night of the raid?"

She hesitated a moment; then her face blanched even whiter. "No," she said almost in a whisper. "I remember

21

he was gone, because he told its afterwards that he had gone to Queen City. He wasn't on the raid."

"Of course he wouldn't tell you what he'd done."

"But you didn't see him. You aren't sure he was there. You don't know Dad, Troy, or you'd know he couldn't do a thing like that. He just couldn't!"

There was no doubting the sincerity in Mary's voice.

"I'm sure about Mike," he said roughly, and jerked his horse around.

CHAPTER 4

THE HITCHRACK IN FRONT OF THE KING'S PALACE was full, but Troy swung down at the end and crowded the horses over, making room for his roan on the outside. He stepped up on the board porch of the saloon and was about to head for the batwings when he noticed a light across the street and a couple of doors in Dr. Holmes' office. Turning, he crossed the dusty street to the office.

Holmes swung away from his desk where he was reading when Troy knocked. Without hesitation he came to the door and swung it back. Troy stepped inside and out of the doorway.

"Oh, it's you," Holmes said in surprise. "I didn't expect to see you in town. Your dad worse?"

"I haven't seen him since you have," Troy said.

The doctor shut the door. "You're looking for Slagg, I suppose. You won't find him here."

"I didn't expect to. But I thought I might pick up some information. Where am I most likely to find Slagg?"

"In the King's Palace, if he's in town."

"That's what I figured. Does he come to town much?"

Holmes nodded. "He'll be here tonight, bragging just like he was this morning."

"How many people know I'm back?"

"If you mean how many have I told, the answer is nobody. A doctor's business is private."

Troy reached for the door knob. "Thanks, Doc. That's what I wanted to know. I'll take my chances from here on."

Troy stepped into the street again. A cool breeze had sprung up, playing gently with the leaves on the cottonwoods in front of the King's Palace.

He pushed through the batwings and paused just to one side of the doors while he looked over the room. The glaring light from the gas lamps swinging over the tables and the bar blinded him for a moment. As his eyes became accustomed to the glare, they pierced the smoke pall hanging over the room.

A bar was on his right, extending almost to the door and curving back against the wall half-way across the long room. Tables were at his left, and several games were in full swing there. Farther back a roulette wheel was spinning, and beyond the bar on the right was a little platform a foot above the level of the floor on which was a piano.

The place was full of men drinking and gambling and adding to the smoke that thickened the air. Troy's entrance had attracted no more than a casual glance or two.

He moved along the bar and made a place for himself at the far end. His back was against the wall, and he could see the entire room and the doors without turning.

The bartender worked his way down the line of customers and finally reached Troy. But Troy only shook his head.

In all the crowded room there was only one face that Troy recognized. That belonged to slim, red-headed Jake Finley. Finley owned a ranch out on the Jericho Hills south of Slagg's place. He had been at the Willoubys' ranch several times before the raid and was about the only man in the valley who had ever pretended to be neighborly. But Finley didn't recognize Troy now, for he barely glanced at him, then turned back to his game. Troy noted that one leg stuck straight out under the table and guessed that it was wooden. He wondered about it. Finley had had both his legs when last he'd seen him, a few days before the Willoubys left the valley.

"Howdy, stranger."

Troy turned to face the big man who had come from the door behind the piano platform. He stood well over six feet, and his dark suit with the open coat accentuated the extra weight he carried on his huge frame. His brown hair, streaked at the temples with grey, had been combed with meticulous care, and his slate gray eyes ran over Troy, sizing him up with slow deliberation. Troy realized that he was looking at King Purdy, owner of the saloon.

"Come far?" Purdy asked.

"Far enough," Troy said. He glanced at the barkeeper and caught his eyes on them. He knew then how it happened that Purdy had suddenly taken an interest in him.

"Looking for somebody?" the big man pressed.

Troy stared into the slate eyes. "Maybe."

"Perhaps I can help you find him."

24

"I'll know him if I see him."

Purdy laid a fat hand on the bar. "We like to make strangers welcome here. Have a drink. It's on the house."

Troy shook his head. "Thanks. I'm just not thirsty tonight."

A frown pulled at Purdy's face; his eyes seemed to lose what little color they had. "We don't like drifters who don't drink in here. They're generally looking for trouble."

Troy jerked his head towards the packed tables. "Looks like a man might get more trouble than he bargained for if he started something in here."

A hint of a smile twitched Purdy's lips. "He would. It's been tried before, and nobody's done any bragging about how lucky they've been."

Purdy turned away towards the door behind the platform. He stopped beside the piano for a moment and looked over the room. Troy saw his head jerk in a slight nod, and glanced out over the crowd to see a small black-haired man turn his dealing over to another and move towards Purdy. The dealer looked at Troy as he passed, and Troy was struck by the light that flashed from his jet black eyes. Beside Purdy, the little man looked like a midget.

The two men passed through the door and closed it, and Troy turned his attention to a girl singer who had just finished her second number and was leaving the platform. She came straight towards Troy as if by prearrangement. Troy saw then that her eyes were hazel and her hair, tied up in front with a red ribbon, was dark brown. She was about his age, maybe a trifle younger.

"You look lonesome, stranger," she said in the same low voice she had used in singing. "Need company?"

"Not particularly," Troy said. "Nice singing."

"Thanks." She smiled. "You didn't listen. You can't even tell me what I sang."

Troy grinned sheepishly. "Maybe not. I had somebody to talk to."

She nodded. "That was the King. And that was his right-hand man, Ace Belling, that you watched go in there with him. Let's introduce ourselves. I'm Kate Brent. I sing here for my bread and butter."

A wild cowboy yell outside cut through the din in the saloon. A dozen pairs of eyes turned towards the doors, but nobody made a move to investigate. Troy turned to the girl, standing rigid beside him.

"Got any idea who the big noise is?"

She nodded, distaste curling the corner of her lips. "One of the worst killers in the valley. Fast with a gun. There's only one man as fast, and that's Ace Belling. If you're figuring on trouble with him, you'd better think again."

"That's according to who it is," Troy said tightly, sensing before she answered that his man was coming.

"It's Cy Slagg, a rancher out close to the Jericho Hills. He's always noisy, but when he whoops it up like that, it means he thinks he's done something unusually smart. He held up the stage this morning and shot old man Willouby."

The batwings slammed inwards, and a big bulk of a man stamped in. His levis, shiny with wear, bore the marks of his trade. His shirt was sweat-soaked and streaked with dirt, and his hat, pushed far back on his head, was coated with the reddish-gray dust of the land over by the Jericho Hills. His pale yellowish eyes swept over the crowded room as he waved an arm towards the bar.

26

"Line up, everybody," he bellowed. "This calls for a celebration. The drinks are on the house. Ain't that right, barkeep?" He roared with laughter at the scowl on the bartender's face.

"You'll have to see the King about that," came the surly reply.

"He ought to be as glad as anybody," Slagg roared. "Everyone in the valley has been scared the Willoubys would come back some day and go on the rampage. They won't do it now. I killed the old he-dog himself this morning. None of the pups will show up."

He slammed his fist on the bar as he looked down the unbroken row of faces crowding every inch of the space facing the sullen bartender. Troy, still in his niche at the end of the bar, saw Purdy and Belling come out of the door behind the piano platform and stand there, watching. Then his gaze centered on Slagg. The time had come, and the lump inside him seemed to reach all the way up into his throat. He felt the sweat standing on his forehead. But his voice was clear and icy cold.

"You might be wrong, Slagg."

Slagg stopped cold, one hand half raised. His eyes fastened on Troy.

"What makes you think so, stranger?" Slagg asked in slow measured tones.

The cold lump was melting in Troy's stomach, now that the waiting was over. He stepped out a foot where he could get a clearer view of Slagg and still keep an eye on everyone in the room. The line of men at the bar had evaporated, leaving Slagg at one end and Troy at the other. Kate had retreated to the piano.

"Look again, Slagg," Troy said. "I'm no stranger to you."

Slagg looked, even taking a couple of steps towards

27

Troy and a step away from the bar. That move took on significance in Troy's mind. Slagg's gun arm was free now. Then suddenly a light began to break across Slagg's broad features.

"You ain't one of the whelps, are you? A Willouby?"

A murmur rippled over the crowd. Troy felt the hot blood pouring through his veins again.

"You're guessing good, Slagg. You didn't have any trouble gunning down an unarmed man today. But it's different now. I'm heeled."

Slagg broke into a bellow of laughter. "So you're heeled?" he roared. There was a bright gleam in his yellow eyes. "Now don't that make it nice? I figured if the Willoubys stayed here, I'd have to hunt them down like snakes, and now I've got them coming to me."

"You're getting your chance, Slagg. You can pull out now and keep on riding."

Incredulity flashed over the big rancher's face; then he broke into another roar of laughter. "Did you hear that?" he demanded of the crowd, and got a sea of grins in response. "He's giving me a chance." His face suddenly darkened. "You came here looking for trouble, Willouby, and when you go out of here, you're going feet first. Make your play."

Troy was tight inside. But his fingers, crooked an inch above his gun, were ready for the lightning move. His indecision was gone. Slagg had taken it away. Destiny had had him in her mould for the past eight years, carefully grooming him for this moment. This was the test. If he failed, there would be no other chance.

"I'm waiting," Troy said. His voice was soft and calm, but it rang through the death-still air like a clarion call.

Slagg hesitated for another second; then, with a bitter curse, dug for his gun. It was a fast draw, but Troy, catching the warning flash in Slagg's eyes, started his move almost simultaneously, and his draw had the perfection that comes from long tiring hours of practice such as few professional gunmen ever get.

Troy fired twice, and squeezed into the split-second between the reports came the roar of Slagg's one shot. But the big rancher was off balance before he pressed the trigger. At the impact of the first slug, utter amazement had wiped the confidence off his face. Slagg's bullet tore a splinter from the floor and slapped it against Troy's leg as he stood watching the big man stagger forward. Two steps he came; then he fell, the gun slipping from his fingers.

For a moment Troy stood looking down at the man. Then with a jerk of his head he motioned to the bartender.

"Crawl over here and get back in the bunch with the rest."

Scowling, the bartender brought his hands up from under the bar and climbed over the mahogany. With the bartender no longer behind his back, Troy turned to face squarely the threat that was rapidly building up in the men.

"Keep your hands in sight," he warned as he began backing cautiously towards the door. He came to Slagg's out-thrust leg and, for a split-second, glanced down to see where he was stepping. In that instant he caught the flash of a gambler's ring in the gaslight.

Troy didn't aim. Instinct, the outgrowth of long tedious hours of practice, guided his shot. The gambler yelled a curse, dropping the derringer he had brought into sight, and grabbed his arm from which blood began

29

to ooze.

"Any more?" Troy asked scathingly, his eyes knifing through the men.

He read fear and hate in most of the faces and admiration in a few. He reached the door. Pursuit would be quick and heated. And in the front row of watchers he saw the man who would lead it. He was shorter than Troy, with glittering blue eyes and a fringe of brown hair ringing his bald head. Two ugly scars made livid paths down one cheek. On his dirty vest a sheriff's star sagged.

"Don't anybody come out of these doors for a full minute," Troy warned sharply. "The man who does is liable to get a dose of lead."

Kicking the doors open, he backed through and dodged around the corner. There he stopped.

The instant he was out of sight, bedlam broke loose inside. A shrill voice that he guessed belonged to the sheriff yapped orders as feet pounded towards the door. Troy knew he could never get to his horse and out of range in time. But there was another way.

The doors slammed open and the sheriff burst out, gun in hand. He stopped with a grunt, dropping his gun, and men behind jammed into him as Troy stepped squarely in front of the officer and poked his gun into his stomach.

"You heard what I said," he snapped. His eyes bored into the men behind the sheriff. "Get back in there or your tin star's a dead man. Move!"

The sheriff croaked a curse. "Hurry, you fools. He'll kill me without blinking."

The men fell back through the doors, and Troy threw another command at them. "Stay there till I'm gone if you want to see this man alive again."

He backed to the end of the hitchrack where his horse stood, pulling the sheriff with him.

"Don't kill me, Willouby," the sheriff whimpered. "I ain't done nothing to you."

Troy looked at the officer's face, pasty gray in the feeble light from the street lamp, and disgust curled his lips. "Don't reckon you're worth killing," he said harshly. "But just make sure you keep on doing nothing to me if you want to stay healthy."

He flipped the reins loose and led his horse down the street past the big pine, keeping the sheriff in step with him. Then, nearly a block from the King's Palace, he swung aboard and kicked the blue roan into a run towards the south.

CHAPTER 5

RIDING TO MAIN STREET, MARY BARSTOW BARELY nodded in response to the elaborate greeting directed her way by Ace Belling. Belling, sleek black hair pasted tight to his head, was standing in the shade of the porch of the King's Palace. He moved to the steps above the street as Mary rode by. Slack business inside, Mary decided, and wished it could always be that way.

But there was always a game when Buddy got in town. Only sixteen, Buddy was supposed to be too young to be allowed in the saloon, but Purdy wouldn't throw him out, and Mike Barstow had lost control of his only son.

Mary kicked her black into a lope, lifting the dust of the street into a curtain between her and the gambler.

She heard her father's voice, loud and threatening and throbbing with anger, as she rode past the house on the way to the barn.

When she had given her horse a handful of oats and opened the back door for him to run into the pasture, she went to the house, hoping the storm was past. The main fury had been spent, but thunder still rumbled from the living-room. She walked quickly, hoping to get through to her room without being drawn into the storm's fury. But Mike, after hammering futile words against the stone ears of his son, turned eagerly to Mary for a sympathetic hearing.

"Know what that worthless brother of yours has done now?" he demanded, his voice thin and ragged with worry and spent anger. "Lost another fifty dollars gambling."

Mary knew how hard that would hit the Barstow budget, and resentment at Buddy and at Ace Belling flared in her. She frowned at her brother. "If you keep on, you'll squander everything we've got."

Buddy twisted his thin sharp features in a show of disgust. "Aw, lay off me, Mary. I had been having a streak of good luck and run ahead a hundred bucks once. I was only trying to get back my luck."

"You know you can't go against gamblers like Ace Belling and win. They're playing you for a sucker."

"That ain't so," Buddy denied hotly. "I won ten dollars one night last week. And just a couple of nights ago I won something I'm going to give to you. It ain't no good to me."

Curiosity pricked Mary, but she ignored it. "I don't want anything you won at gambling."

Buddy grinned confidently. "Youll want this, all right."

Mike Barstow rubbed his chin, a nervous gesture that was becoming a habit with him. "Is it worth fifty

32

dollars?"

Buddy looked at Mike defiantly. "Maybe. I don't know. But I'm giving it to Mary. That's the only reason I played for it. I put up twenty dollars against it."

"Twenty dollars on one hand?" Mike bellowed. "You lunatic!"

"I figure it's worth it," Buddy said easily. "Look." He reached into his pocket and brought out a little sack and carefully opened it, holding up his prize.

"A string of beads!" Mike said disgustedly.

Mary's determination to have nothing to do with Buddy's winnings melted as she saw the necklace dangling from her brother's hand. Almost involuntarily she moved over, her fingers reaching out.

"Here, Sis," Buddy said. "Take a good look."

Mary took the necklace almost reverently. It was a short necklace, just long enough to reach around the throat. Strung together were little heart-shaped mountings that looked like gold. And on each gold heart was a glittering brilliant.

"Diamonds," Mary breathed.

"Diamonds?" Mike roared. "Huh! "He picked up his hat and stamped out of the house.

Buddy grinned. "Guess you're a little excited about them things being diamonds, Sis. They're just pretty glass, I reckon. But they were worth putting up twenty bucks for. They're all yours now."

"Thank you, Buddy. But I shouldn't take them. Not if you won them gambling."

"Why not? I won them fair and square. I can do what I want to with them."

Buddy reached for his hat and hurriedly left the house.

Mary went to her room, walking like one in a dream.

33

Never had she seen anything so richly beautiful or so dazzling as the necklace.

She fastened it around her throat and admired it in the mirror. It would be the foundation of a thousand new dreams into which she could escape when worries piled too high.

She heard Mike stamp back into the house and go into the little room where he kept his private things. He liked to call it his office. Faintly she heard voices and realized that Mike had company.

Suddenly she realized it was nearly supper time. She should be helping her mother. Mrs. Barstow must have been in the garden gathering lettuce for supper when she came home. It would take time to wash that and get it ready to serve along with the rest of the meal.

Carefully, she laid the necklace in the back of the little drawer on top of her bureau and went out into the living-room. The voices from the office reached her and slowed her steps, pulling her thoughts from Buddy's gift. She recognized Ed Swazey's voice arguing with Mike. Swazey was a frequent visitor at the Barstows', and today his voice was honed thin with excitement.

"I don't like it any better than you do, Mike," Swazey was saying. "But it's our only chance."

"I ain't cut out for that kind of killing," Mike said heavily. "Not in the back, anyway."

"Ain't either one of us fast enough with a gun to do it any other way," Swazey argued. "As for killing, you'd have a hard time convincing some people you can't do that."

"I know. You don't have to remind me. But I ain't going to backshoot young Willouby."

"If you don't kill him, he'll get you. You know that."

"Maybe. Maybe not. I ain't dead yet."

The voice went on, but Mary shut her ears and rushed blindly through the room and out under the cottonwoods west of the house.

CHAPTER 6

DISMOUNTING AT THE ROCK, TROY GLANCED AT HIS watch. Nearly ten o'clock, the time the doctor had set for meeting him here. For a time he knew doubt whether the doctor would come. After all, it probably wouldn't increase his popularity if it was discovered he was doctoring a Willouby. But that doubt was dispersed when he saw the doctor's horse coming acress the flat from town. Caution made Troy pull his horse around behind the rock and wait. When the doctor reined up, he stepped into view.

"Howdy, Doc. Alone?"

Holmes, startled by Troy's sudden appearance, frowned. "Did you expect me to bring an army?"

"There are some in Big Pine who would do about that if they had your chance."

"Your secret is safe with me. So far as I'm concerned, a patient's private life is his own business so long as it doesn't interfere with his recovery. Let's get going."

Troy produced his blindfold. "How are things in town?"

Holmes frowned at the blindfold, then shrugged. "Hotter than a toad on a skillet. You made quite a reputation for yourself the other night. Also got a price on your head. You're a bit unpopular in certain circles in town."

"Why the price on my head?"

35

"Sheriff Emitt calls you a dangerous criminal and has offered five hundred dollars of county funds to anyone bringing you in."

"Easy money for somebody."

The doctor's lips twiched. "I didn't notice anybody starting on the hunt."

Troy tied the blindfold in place, feeling again the wave of guilt at the action. But five hundred dollars might look good even to a doctor.

It seemed to Troy that time dragged as he led the doctor's horse up the trail bordering Deer Creek. Inactivity was wearing him down. Patience had been one thing he had failed to develop while preparing himself for his return to Storm Valley. Now he must overcome that weakness.

Boone was waiting at the mouth of the cave and helped the doctor step down. Eagerness was in his face when Troy lifted the blindfold and turned the doctor towards Dan.

The examination was short but thorough. Holmes redressed the wound and took Dan's temperature. Finally he put the instruments back in his little satchel and stood up.

"How is he, Doc?" Boone asked, eyes flashing. "How soon can we get out of here?"

"He's tougher than a boiled owl," Holmes said. "Otherwise he'd be dead. He'll be ready to take on an army single-handed before you know it."

Boone gripped the doctor's arm. "Can we get him out in the next day or two?"

Holmes frowned. "Hold on now, kid. Don't push your luck. Your dad is gaining fast, but it will be several weeks before it's safe to move him."

"Weeks?" The word came from Boone like a hollow echo.

"You're still lucky," the doctor said. "He came within a whisper of cashing in. I'll come back in a couple of days to see him again."

Troy tied on the blindfold, furtively watching his brother. He felt sorry for Boone, for the youngster had no heart for the thing they had come here to do.

"I've got some business in town," Troy said as he started down the trail leading the doctor's horse. "I'll be back before night."

Boone nodded, disappointment pulling down his round face.

At the big rock when Troy took off the blindfold, the doctor blinked at him from under lowered brows. "Next time you can leave that rag in your pocket. I've got enough of bouncing over that trail without seeing where I'm going."

Troy grinned. The doctor's temper was rubbed raw by his ride; he had a right to be on the prod. "Okay, Doc. I reckon I've got to trust somebody, and you look like the best bet. I'll meet you here day after tomorrow and lead you in without the blinder. All I ask is that you don't tell anyone how to get to us, and be mighty careful when you come that nobody follows you."

Holmes nodded. "That's fair enough."

Troy checked the doctor as he started to rein towards town. "Where's the courthouse in Big Pine?"

Holmes looked sharply at Troy. "There isn't any courthouse yet. The offices are wherever they are handiest. Pretty poor system, if ,you ask me. Purdy was elected treasurer, and he keeps everything safe in his safe in the Palace. His office is in the back of the saloon. A man named Jeffries is clerk and holds sway in the sheriff's office whenever he's on the job. That's one day a week. The rest of the time he's up in the Jericho Hills looking for gold."

"Where are the county records?"

"In Sheriff Emitt's safe, I suppose. They're where you won't get to see them, if that's what you're thinking of."

"Why not?"

"The sheriff's office is hardly the place for you to walk into with a price on your head."

Troy nodded. "I might surprise the tin star, at that. I'll try to keep our parley quiet, but if it gets out of hand, it may drum up some business for you. Better get going, Doc. I don't want to come in town too close on your heels."

Troy built a smoke and lit it while the doctor loped towards town.

He ground out his cigarette on the saddle horn and lifted the reins. The doctor was out of sight at the creek crossing by Barstow's place. He would be in town well ahead of Troy.

After crossing Storm Creek, Troy swung his blue roan off the trail and struck into the willows that bordered Pine Creek, a half-mile above the spot where it emptied into the bigger stream. Following the trees, he kept out of sight until he was even with the town. There he left his horse tied to a low limb. It was less than fifty yards to the first buildings and only a half block from there to the back of the buildings facing Main Street. One of these was the sheriff's office; there was a little one-cell jail in the back.

Troy moved quickly across the open space to the first building, a little shack much in need of paint and repair. From there he walked boldly along the side of the sheriff's office and stepped up on the boardwalk running the length of Main Street.

Across from Troy was a hotel, the largest building in town. It was there the stage made its stop. At an angle across the street a block away, he saw Dr. Holmes leaning in his doorway, watching the sheriff's office, alert now that he had spotted Troy. Troy glanced down the street towards the King's Palace, then turned through the door.

There was one man in the room. He was leaning back in his chair behind the desk, hat pulled over his eyes, asleep. A soft breeze coming through the open window by the desk ruffled some papers held down by a heavy gun belt.

Troy stepped to one side of the door. "You've got company, Sheriff."

The front legs of Emitt's chair thumped on the floor and the sheriff rubbed a hand over his face and back over his shiny pate, knocking his hat to the floor. The last shred of sleep evaporated from his eyes as he squinted at his visitor.

"Willouby!" he breathed. His hand shot forward towards the gun on his desk, but he stopped as he looked into the bore of Troy's gun.

"I think we'll have a quieter talk if I take that gun." Troy reached forward, jerked the gun belt off the desk and stuck the gun in his waistband, tossing the belt in the corner. "Where are the county records?"

"In my safe," Emitt snapped. "Nobody sees them unless Jeffries says so."

"It's going to be different today. Open the safe."

"What is this? A hold-up?"

"Call it whatever you like. You've got a price on my head, anyway. Open up your safe." He jerked his head

39

towards the safe standing in the corner behind the desk.

Emitt didn't move. "That's county business."

Troy stepped closer to the desk. "You're not worth any more to me than Slagg was. If you want the same as he got, just keep on being stubborn."

The color faded from Emitt's face, and he retreated before Troy's gun until his back was against the safe. "Okay, Willouby. You've got the upper hand this time."

"I aim to keep it," Troy snapped. "Get busy."

The sheriff turned to the safe, and Troy glanced out the door. The street was quiet now, but someone might appear at any minute. And almost everyone, except Dr. Holmes, could be classed as an enemy now.

The safe door swung open, and Troy stepped around the desk. "Get over by the door," he ordered. "And keep your hands in sight."

Troy crouched beside the open safe door and sorted through the papers, carefully checking Emitt's moves out of the corner of his eye. His fingers struck a book, thicker than the other papers, and he lifted it out. One glance at the cover told him he had found the record of land deeds.

Taking the book to the desk, he flipped it open and glanced over the entries, raising his eyes to check every move Emitt made. Then he found what he was looking for and scanned it quickly.

He looked up at the sheriff. "How did Barstow get a deed to his ranch just three years after we left?"

"Sheriff's sale. It was sold for taxes."

"Taxes!" Troy exploded. "In three years?"

"Rules of the county," Emitt said, unruffled. "The county was new and needed money bad. The commissioners ruled that land with three years' back taxes due must be sold to get the money."

40

"Who were the commissioners?"

"Jake Finley, Ed Swazey, and Mike Barstow."

Troy nodded. "Just like I thought." He looked again at the record.

"This record isn't very complete. How much did Barstow pay at the sale?"

"Five hundred dollars, if it's any of your business."

Troy nodded. A tenth of what the ranch was worth. Troy needed no more proof of Mike Barstow's guilt. He reached down to close the book. It was then he noticed the shadow darken the room. His eyes leaped to the open door. Red-headed Jake Finley stood there, his gun muzzle covering Troy. A wide triumphant grin spread over his face, a face made red by big blotches of freckles.

"Let go of your gun easy," Finley ordered.

Troy let his fingers relax, and his gun dropped to the top of the desk. Quickly he weighed his chances and found them overbalanced by Finley's unwavering gun. His one chance was to make a break. For once he was disarmed and in that cell behind him, he knew he would never come out alive.

"What's eating you, Jake?" he asked slowly, stalling for time to find a loophole. "You used to be friendly to the Willoubys—about the only friend we had."

"Things have been peaceful since you left. They ain't now. And I like peace. Frisk him, Eli. Then lock him up."

"Sure." The sheriff's shrill voice rose in triumph. He came towards the desk like a, released spring. It was then Troy saw his chance.

Emitt was unarmed and, in his excitement, he had crossed between Finley and Troy. Troy's hands, an inch above the desk top, suddenly darted down, gripped the

41

edge of the desk and heaved. Emitt squalled a warning as he tried to dodge, but he was too late. The desk hit him and slammed him back against Finley. The record book and Emitt's papers scattered over the floor.

Troy spun around and, gripping the sheriff's gun in his waistband, dived through the open window. He landed on his knees and rolled over. Instantly he was on his feet and racing down the alley towards his horse in the willows on the creek bank.

He was past the last house before a shot was fired. The bullet kicked up the sod at his feet and he ducked sideways, bringing the little shack between him and the sheriff's office.

He heard the men shouting for horses back in town as he reached the willows. But with his rangy roan under him, Troy had little fear of pursuit. He crossed the creek and headed west, leading the chase away from the cave.

CHAPTER 7

IMPATIENCE GNAWED AT TROY AS HE NEARED THE BIG rock below the look-out to meet the doctor on his next visit.

For two days he had scarcely left the cave except to go up to the look-out to watch the sheriff and his posse scour the valley for trace of him.

As before, the doctor was on time and, with little more than a greeting, Troy led the way back along the Deer Creek trail to the cave. The examination of the wounded man was short, and Holmes came out into the sunlight nodding his approval.

"In a few days you can move him out in the sun in the morning," he said. "He's gaining fast." He fastened his little bag on his saddle and picked up the reins. Then he turned back to Troy. "I've got a message for you."

"If it's from the sheriff, I'm not interested."

"It's not from Emitt. It's from Ace Belling."

Troy's cold gray eyes bored into the doctor. "Belling? How did he know you'd be seeing me?"

"Any smart man could figure out where I've been these days after I close my office and leave town."

"Anybody try to follow you?"

"I don't think so. Your brother keeps a look-out, doesn't he?"

Troy nodded. Holmes was observant enough to be a detective. "What did Belling want?"

"He wants to have a talk with you, alone. Says he's got a deal to offer you, one that you're sure to like."

"What kind of a deal could Belling make with me?"

"I'm not a fortune-teller. And Belling's pretty tight-lipped. He wouldn't have said anything to me if he could have found any other way of getting word to you. Shall I tell him youre interested?"

Troy thought of the sleek-haired, dapper gambler. If Belling had a proposition to make, it was a cinch he saw an advantage in it for himself. Still, there might be something for Troy to gain, too. Anything would be better than just waiting.

"Where does he want to meet me?"

"He suggested the old Nelson place. That's somewhere down Storm Creek towards the Jericho Hills."

Troy nodded. "I know where it is. Nelson was living there when we left. Must be he didn't toe the mark laid down by the bosses."

"Maybe. I wouldn't know about that." Holmes swung into the saddle. "Belling will want to know."

"I'll talk to him. When?"

"Four this afternoon." The doctor leaned from his saddle. "I'll give you a word of advice. Don't trust Ace Belling. He's as tricky as a fox."

"Thanks, Doc. I've already got him pegged. I wouldn't trust him any farther than I could throw a bull by the tail."

The doctor reined away. "I reckon you can take care of yourself. I'll be back in a few days."

Troy turned into the cave to stir up the fire and get dinner started. Boone would be back down from the look-out soon. But dinner couldn't keep Troy's mind off his rendezvous this afternoon. Belling must have a reason, a good one, for wanting such a meeting. But Troy could find only one logical possibility. The gambler might be a tool of Emitt's to lure Troy out into the open. That was a chance Troy had to take.

Leaving the cave just after noon, Troy was out in the valley riding towards the old Nelson cabin two hours before the appointed time. If there was a trap being set, he wanted to be on hand to see it prepared.

Although he was far ahead of time, he approached the deserted cabin with caution. Nelson had built his cabin close to the creek and had set out some cottonwoods for glade. In front of the door he had transplanted two pines from the slopes of Storm Range. These had grown well and, with the cottonwoods and the willows that grew uninvited along the banks of the river, made a little forest around the cabin. Troy wondered why anyone would want to leave such a place. But then the Willoubys hadn't wanted to leave their place, either.

Tying his horse in the willows two hundred yards

from the cabin, he advanced on foot. From a vantage point on the river bank, for ten minutes he watched the cabin and the surrounding trees for a sign of movement before venturing towards the pines guarding the door.

At the door he hesitated again. Something could happen when he lifted the latch and swung the door open. Emitt might be that tricky. But there was only one way to find out. The best place to wait for Belling would be inside the cabin looking out.

He jerked the latch up and with a kick sent the door in. A tide of musty air swept out. Cautiously, gun in hand, he moved inside. Nelson apparently hadn't been gone many months. The windows were still intact and the door worked well on its hinges. Nothing had been inside to disturb the dust on the floor or on the few pieces of furniture still remaining—a broken chair, a table too wobbly to be worth moving, and a badly battered stove.

Shoving the door shut, Troy brushed the dust from the stove top and seated himself where he could look through the dingy windows and see the trails approaching the cabin from both directions. He sat there for an hour.

As the time drew near for Belling to appear, Troy began to have his doubts that the gambler would come at all. But the fear of a trap faded. Emitt, he was sure, would rather spring a surprise on him than try to smoke him out after he had established himself.

He saw Belling coming down towards the cabin on the trail leading from town. Belling was a good rider for a man who spent most of his time indoors. He rode to the front of the cabin and swung down, striding towards the door. Troy's muscles tightened; his hand was on his gun. Without any preliminaries, the door swung open and Belling stood there, grinning confidently.

"Thought you'd be here," he said.

"That's a good way to get a slug in your belly," Troy said testily.

"Why so? We had a date to meet here. You saw me coming."

"How did you know I was here?"

"I investigated a little and found your horse down in the willows. Where else would you be but here where you could get the drop on anybody coming in?"

"You didn't bring any company?"

Belling came into the room. "I didn't need company on this trip. The sheriff is on the other side of town this afternoon."

"I thought he might be with you."

"I ain't fool enough to put my chips on a dead man. And that's what you'd be if Emitt got a chance at you."

Troy left the stove and crossed to a window. "So you want to put some chips on me?"

"I've got a proposition to make. There's no place in it for the sheriff."

"What's the proposition?" Troy turned to face Belling.

"You do a little chore for me and I'll give you the names of the men on that raid eight years ago."

Suspicion squinted Troy's eyes. "What makes you think I don't already know who the men on that raid were?"

Belling laughed. "You don't. If you did, there would have been two new graves out in Boothill instead of one."

Belling's meaning struck Troy. Still he stalled, drawing out the gambler. "Meaning?"

"Slagg wasn't the only member of that raiding party

who was in the King's Palace that night. You wouldn't have missed the chance of lowering the odds against you if you'd known. How about making a deal?"

"What kind of a job do you want me to do?"

"It won't put you out any. Just get rid of a couple of the men on your list right now."

"Why the hurry?"

Belling grinned, his eyes failing to hide their cunning. "That's my business. I don't tell you how to get rid of the men you're after, and you don't pry into my affairs. You can shove them out of the valley or give them a one way ticket to Boothill. That's up to you."

"Why don't you kill your own snakes?"

"I do if it's necessary. But this time it isn't. You're here to get rid of these particular snakes, so why should I cut in on your deal?"

Troy had to admit it sounded reasonable. But there was more that the gambler wasn't telling. And he wasn't going to tell. The proposition was there. Troy could take it or leave it. On the face of it, there was nothing for him to lose. But there must be some urgent reason for Belling wanting to get somebody out of the valley, or he wouldn't make such an offer. Or perhaps there was some other angle behind the gambler's offer. Either way, Troy couldn't see that he had anything to lose. At least it would give him a lead to work on.

"Give me the names."

Belling grinned triumphantly. "You'll live up to your end of the bargain?"

"You know why I came back to Storm Valley," Troy said slowly. "That ought to be answer enough for you."

Belling hesitated, then nodded. "There were six men on the raid."

"Seven," Troy corrected him.

47

The gambler frowned at Troy. "Six is all I heard about. Reckon there could have been another one."

"How did you find out who was on the raid?"

Belling laughed. "Don't get ideas. I wasn't in the bunch. I got my information from Slagg. He would come into the Palace, get a little tight, and shoot off his mouth. He bragged about his part in the raid more than once. From what he said, I got six names."

"Whom did he name beside Barstow and himself?" Troy demanded impatiently.

"Barstow was the leader. Then there were the Swazey boys and Slagg himself and Ross Hale, the old codger who lives over under Hermit Peak. And the other one he named was Eli Emitt."

Surprise rocked Troy as he considered the last name. But it was gone in a second. Emitt's eagerness to get rid of him might not stem wholly from his sense of duty as sheriff. And if Barstow's gang was the real power in the valley, the sheriff's office would be under Barstow's control.

"You don't know the other name?" Troy pressed.

Belling shook his head. "Those were the only ones Slagg ever mentioned. I supposed that was all. Now for your part, I want you to get rid of Mike Barstow and Ross Hale immediately."

"Why the rush?"

"I told you that was my business. You don't have to kill them if you're chicken-hearted. But get them out of this valley." He turned towards the door. "I wouldn't advise you to loaf around town much. Emitt is a pretty fair shot."

Troy watched him mount and ride back up the trail towards Big Pine.

From one of the two shelves built along one wall of the cabin, he tore a wide piece of wrapping paper that had been used to cover the shelf. Digging into his pocket, he brought out a stub pencil he had carried there since he left Texas. Laying the paper on the rickety table, he carefully listed the six names Belling had given him, putting Mike Barstow at the head and leaving a long blank line at the bottom. Then he crossed off Hal Swazey's and Cy Slagg's names. Folding the paper, he stuffed it in his pocket and went outside, cutting down through the willows to his horse.

It was sundown when he reached Pine Creek and turned to follow it towards town. To suit his plans, it had to be pitch dark when he hit Big Pine, so he stepped down and loosened the cinch on his roan.

Two hours later he mounted again and followed the willows to the spot behind the sheriff's office where he had left his horse a couple of days before. Tying his roan, he moved up past the jail to the front of the building.

The street was noisy down in front of the King's Palace and the other saloon, but almost deserted here. Moving out on the street, he stepped up to the door of the sheriff's office. Flipping the folds out of the paper he dug from his pocket, he ripped a hole in it above the list of names he had written and shoved it over the door knob. He looked up and down the street to see if he had been noticed, then dodged back into the alley between the sheriff's office and the blacksmith shop on the corner of the block.

He waited long enough to satisfy himself there would be no activity in this end of town before morning, then turned towards the willows to spend the night. He would be back early in the morning to see Emitt when he found the list on his door. Then he would know for certain if Belling had told the truth in naming the sheriff.

CHAPTER 8

THE NIGHT HAD GIVEN TROY LITTLE REST. BUT HIS eyes and ears were keen as he waited for the first stirring from the town. Crouching behind a barrel filled with rubbish and scraps from the blacksmith shop, he wondered how long he would have to wait for Emitt to appear at his office.

The town woke early. But the sun was well over the buildings across the street before Troy saw Emitt come from the hotel opposite the sheriff's office. A toothpick hung from one corner of his mouth, and as he crossed the dusty street, he sprinkled some Duke's Mixture into a brown cigarette paper. Spitting out the toothpick, he sealed the cigarette and stopped on the walk in front of his office to light it.

With the match in front of his face, he froze, looking over his cupped hand at the paper on his door knob. Troy couldn't follow his movements as he stepped forward. But he was close enough to hear Emitt's surprised curses. Then his voice rose to a bellow that summoned the town, and Troy thought he detected a note of fear mingled with the rage.

The blacksmith, who had just opened his shop, came on the run. Emitt stamped out to meet him, waving the paper he had taken from the door. Troy got a good look at the sheriff's face, and it was enough to convince him that Belling had not been lying when he had put Emitt's name on the list of the guilty. The sheriff's face had lost

50

its color, his cigarette was gone, and his eyes had the wild desperate look of a boy caught in an orchard with his pockets full of apples.

A storekeeper and a barber joined the blacksmith to look at the list that Emitt held. As more men came in response to Emitt's outburst, the sheriff regained his courage, bolstering it with the security born of numbers. Finally, in response to a rising question, he wheeled towards his office with a great show of bravado.

"I'll show you what I'm going to do," he bawled. "Just wait and you'll see."

The men waited, and Troy had to stay in his low crouch because some of them were directly in front of the alley where Troy was hiding. He heard Emitt stamp out of his office; the men crowded forward. One of them read aloud what Emitt had written on the paper.

Emitt started making wild threats and finally led the men towards the King's Palace to drink to the imminent end of the Willoubys.

When the last of the men had left the front of the office, Troy rose from his crouch and kicked the kinks out of his legs. He was just turning to make a run for the willows and his horse when he heard hoofbeats out in the street. There was no time to make a run for it. All he could do was sink down behind the barrel again.

He saw Mary drop from her horse and run to the door of the office. But his surprise at sight of the girl in town this early was swallowed by the amazement that struck him as his eyes caught the sparkle of her necklace. He was too far away to be positive of what he had seen. But he couldn't still the excitement that surged through him.

Mary came back towards her horse, and Troy dodged out to intercept her. He talked rapidly, for he caught movement down in front of the King's Palace. One man

51

came out, then darted back, and a second later another man stepped out on the porch. The latter wasn't in such a hurry, and Troy recognized him as the gambler, Ace Belling. It wouldn't be more than a minute till the town would be swarming with men after his scalp.

The instant Troy got Mary's promise to meet him in the cottonwoods, he ducked back into the alley as men streamed out of the saloon. He made a dash for his horse in the willows along Pine Creek and was almost there when he heard the sheriff's roar and knew the hound was on the scent.

Troy rode down the stream towards its junction with Storm Creek, stopping at intervals to listen for sounds of pursuit. Finally he stopped to listen once more before cutting out of the willows. It was then that he heard a twig crack ahead of him and whirled, his hand whipping his gun from its holster.

"Never mind the gun," Belling said easily, his hands outspread.

Troy let his gun drop back into leather. "What's the idea, Belling?"

"I wanted to have a little talk with you."

Troy watched the gambler closely. "What have you got to say?"

"That was a crazy stunt you pulled—posting up that list, then waiting in town till everybody saw it."

"I found out what I wanted to know."

"Didn't believe me when I named Emitt. Is that it?"

"Did you expect me to?"

Belling shook his head. "Maybe you do now. I'm too smart to give you a bum steer. And I was smart enough to figure out what you were up to and cut you off here while Emitt was still turning the town upside down hunting for you."

Troy saw the pride in the gambler's face. "Is that all you rode out here to tell me?"

"No. You seemed mighty familiar with Mary. Don't get any ideas. She's my girl. Understand?"

"Maybe."

Ross Hale's cabin, a poorly built affair, stood fifty yards back from the creek. Some scraggly pines grew close to either side of it, and the high wall that formed one side of the notch through which Storm Creek escaped into the valley rose just behind the shack.

At the fringe of trees bordering the open area between the cabin and the creek, Troy stopped. Better not crowd the old codger. Troy remembered him as a surly, mysterious old man, one he'd been afraid of as a boy.

Suddenly, as if just released, two big heavy-boned hounds charged out of the cabin door. They came halfway to Troy before they hit the end of their chains. They lunged against the chains, and Troy could see the eagerness, in their blazing eyes. They were trained to kill.

Then the old man appeared in the doorway, a rifle swinging from the crook of his arm. His hair and full beard were iron gray, and deep crow's-feet stretched out from both eyes, eyes so light blue they were almost colorless.

"What do you want?" he demanded in a sharp shrill voice, squirting tobacco juice through yellow snags of teeth.

"I wanted to talk to you," Troy shouted above the bay of the hounds. "I'm Willouby."

Hale jerked his head in a nod. "I know who you are. I know everybody in the valley." He gave a sharp command to the dogs, and they ceased their clamor and turned obediently back into the house. "Light and come in."

Troy swung down, tied his horse to a tree limb and advanced slowly.

Stepping inside the shack, he was met by the steady baleful glares of the two dogs, one standing on each side of the crude table. He looked at the old man and drove straight to the point of his visit.

"I suppose you remember us Willoubys and why we left the valley."

"And I know why you're back. You got a good start on your job by plugging Slagg."

"I was given a list of the men who were on that raid," Troy stated. "Your name is on that list."

Hale's laugh came instantly, a shrill cackle that traveled down Troy's spine like a drop of cold water on a hot day.

"I ain't surprised I was named. I could tell you who gave you the list, I reckon. And I could name every man that was on that raid, too. There were seven."

Troy nodded. "That's right: seven. Who were they?"

Hale laughed again. "I ain't telling nothing unless there's something in it for me. But I can tell you for sure I wasn't there."

"Then how do you know who was?"

"I make it my business to know things." He grinned, showing his yellow snags and letting tobacco juice leak out over his thin lips to trickle down into stained whiskers. "That's how I get along."

"Blackmail?"

The old man cackled. "Call it what you like. If anybody wants to know anything bad enough, they pay me what I ask and I tell them. There ain't nothing in this valley that I don't know." He waved a hand at the dogs. "Me and the dogs find out everything."

54

Troy considered asking the price the old miser wanted for revealing the names, but the thought of buying his information rankled.

"How do I know you wouldn't lie to me?"

"You don't. But I ain't got no reason to lie. Just put up enough to make it worth while."

"How much would that be?"

"More than I'm being paid to keep quiet."

Troy tried to see behind the colorless eyes and failed. "You'd double-cross somebody else to tell me?"

"I ain't double-crossing nobody. I just sell to the highest bidder. If you're it, I'll tell you. If you ain't, I won't."

Troy sized up the old man. He saw nothing there to trust. "I think I'll find out myself."

"That's up to you, Willouby. I ain't talking unless I'm paid."

"What if I keep your name on my list?"

"You'll be wrong," Hale said easily. Then he looked at his dogs and grinned. "I ain't worrying none."

Troy stepped through the door and started towards his horse. Hale followed him outside. "If you change your mind, come back."

Part way to his horse, Troy heard the old man give a grunt. There was a rattle of chains, and Troy wheeled in time to see the dogs catapult through the door. He leaped towards his horse, and the dogs hit the ends of their chains several feet short of him. The hermit's shrill cackle echoed over the clearing.

"Just something to think about, Willouby," he said. Troy swung up and reined downstream.

CHAPTER 9

THE SUN WASN'T YET NOON-HIGH WHEN TROY LEFT Hale's shack. He thought of going back to the cave but decided against it. The fewer times he rode in and out on the trail to the cave, the safer their hide-out would remain. And tonight he had a date to keep in the cottonwoods at Barstow's.

Finding a shady spot along the creek bank where he ran little risk of being seen, he reined up and unsaddled the roan. From a saddle bag, he brought out a sack of dried peaches which he always carried. The peaches and some raisins made up his dinner.

Thinking about the necklace Mary had been wearing but more about Mary herself, he dropped off to sleep. When he roused, the sun was tipping Hermit Peak, giving the valley a parting caress. Troy waited impatiently for darkness. When the twilight had deepened to thick dusk, he saddled his roan and moved down the creek bank.

Darkness was complete when he came in sight of the light blinking from Barstow's kitchen window. Reining away from the creek, he rode to the edge of the cottonwoods and dismounted. He tied the roan and moved forward into the grove to wait.

He saw Mary as soon as she left the house, for she was dressed in white and the little sliver of moon hanging in the western half of the sky pointed her out in sharp relief against the rigid lines of the building.

When she was within ten yards of him he moved away from the trunk of a big cottonwood where he had been leaning. At first move, she stopped, and he heard her catch her breath.

"You were looking for me, weren't you?" Troy asked as he stepped towards her.

"Yes," she admitted. "But you startled me."

Her voice was low, little more than a whisper. Troy stopped as she moved over against the bole of a tree. The moonlight cut through the leaves to lay a checkered pattern of light and shadow on her hair and face.

"You've got the wrong idea, Troy," she said. "Dad wasn't on that raid."

"I can't agree with you on that."

"Where did you get that list?"

"What difference does it make where I got it? So far I've found it to be right."

"You haven't checked it," she cried. "If you had, you'd know Dad is innocent."

"I was checking it this morning. If you'd seen Emitt's face when he found that list, you'd have known he was guilty."

"Maybe Emitt. I wouldn't put anything past him. But not Dad." She moved closer to Troy, laying a hand on his arm. "Please, Troy, don't do something you'll be sorry for."

Silently Troy cursed the giddiness that swept over him at the girl's touch.

"I won't be sorry for what I do," he said roughly to cover up his shakiness.

"You would be if you punished the wrong man."

"I won't."

"Then you'll not touch Dad," she cried. Her hand gripped tighter on his arm. "Promise me you won't, Troy."

"I made a promise to myself to even the score for what happened years ago. That still stands."

"I'm not asking you to change that. Just don't harm Dad. He isn't guilty."

"All right, Mary," he said, his voice choked down to a whisper. "I promise."

She squeezed his arm tighter before letting go and stepping back. "Thank you, Troy. You won't be sorry." Her fingers reached up to caress the necklace at her throat. "You said something this morning about this necklace. Was that why you wanted to see me tonight?"

Troy got a grip on himself again, rubbing a hand over his forehead as he tried to still the hammering of heart.

"Yes. I wanted to ask you where you got it."

"My brother gave it to me," she said, and he thought he detected a tinge of embarrassment in her voice.

"Where did he get it?" Troy pressed.

"He won it gambling. From Ace Belling."

The name struck Troy a hard blow. He knew Mary's brother couldn't be much over sixteen. Hardly a seasoned enough gambler to win anything valuable from a veteran like Ace Belling. But if he hadn't won It...

"How did he happen to win that from Belling?"

Mary's voice dropped to a whisper. "Just lucky, I guess."

He knew then. Belling had said she was his girl. But he hadn't believed him. He fought down an impulse to get away as quickly as possible.

"Where did Belling get it?"

"From a gambler passing through, he said."

"He told you that himself?" Condemnation was in Troy's voice.

She nodded, then moved a step closer to him. "Ace didn't give me the necklace," she said softly. "Honest.

Buddy won it and gave it to me."

Troy didn't say anything for a moment, fighting the sickness that swept over him.

"Maybe Belling made it easy for your brother to win. He said you were his girl."

"I'm sorry, Troy."

Anger at himself flamed up, momentarily burning out the pain. Why should he care what a Barstow did? It was nothing to him. He was a fool to let it affect him.

"Why should you be sorry?" he snapped. "It's your life. What more could a man expect from a Barstow?"

He saw the agony on her face, and the savage satisfaction he had taken in hurting her vanished as he saw how completely he had succeeded.

Wheeling, he cut through the grove towards his horse, stumbling over sticks and getting slapped in the face with low limbs.

He reached his horse and mounted, still distraught. It was only after he was on his roan and moving towards the river, fifty yards distant, that he became aware of the other horse racing west along the river bank.

Like a bolt of lightning it struck him that trouble was probably riding on that horse. Without another second's hesitation, he wheeled his roan and put him on the trail of the fleeing rider.

Barstow's cottonwood grove fell behind as the chase led up the river bank towards Hale's shack. Troy wondered if it was Hale ahead.

Gradually the roan shortened the distance between Troy and the leading rider. Troy rode low, offering as little a target as possible for any lead the other might unleash at him. But no shots came, and Troy became convinced as he closed in that the other was unarmed. Within ten yards of the horseman, Troy shouted a warning:

"Pull up if you don't want a slug in your back."

There was no hesitation in the other's move. He hauled up on the reins and slid to a halt so fast that Troy had to pull in sharply to keep from overrunning him. Wheeling, he got his first look at the rider. It wasn't Hale as he had expected.

"What's the hurry, Swazey?" he asked.

Ed Swazey twisted in his saddle uncomfortably. "I was on my home from town when I saw you come out of the cottonwoods, and I didn't want any trouble. That's all."

Troy's gaze searched Swazey. The man had no gun.

"Kind of careless of you not to be packing a gun, don't you think?" Troy said.

Swazey's eyes widened in fear. "I ain't looking for trouble."

"Being caught without any hardware doesn't always keep you out of trouble."

A whimper crept into Swazey's voice. "They said you wouldn't shoot an unarmed man."

Troy watched the fear in the man's eyes and heard the panicky sob in his voice. Troy's voice was hard. "You're a yellow-livered coward, Swazey. I'm going to let you go now. But you'd better be far from this valley by tomorrow night or else, the next time you see me, start smoking. I won't wait to see if you've got a gun."

"Sure, Willouby," Swazey said eagerly. "Sure."

He lifted his horse into a run for a hundred yards, then slowed to turn into a ford across Storm Creek. A mile south of the ford was Swazey's little run-down ranch. He wouldn't have much to leave behind, Troy thought.

Troy turned back slowly. He could cross off another

name. For Swazey wouldn't be here when the sun went down again.

It was nearing midnight when Troy unsaddled and hobbled his horse and went into the cave. He expected both Boone and Dan to be asleep, but a challenging voice came out of the darkness.

"That you, Troy?"

"Yeah." Troy moved towards the voice. "Anything you want, Dad?"

"I want to talk to you. Get a light going."

Troy struck a match, lit the candle and sat down close to Dan.

"Where have you been?" Dan demanded.

"Down in the valley. Got the names of some more who were on that raid."

Dan pushed up on an elbow. "Who?" he demanded, his eyes sparkling.

"Emitt, the sheriff, for one. And Ross Hale was named. But I'm not sure about him."

"Who told you?"

"The gambler, Ace Belling. I'm not too fond of Belling, but I checked on part of the list he gave me, and I know that much is right."

Dan leaned forward. "Did he name all seven?"

Troy shook his head. "Only six. And I'm not certain about all of them. I met Swazey tonight and gave him till tomorrow to get out of the country."

Dan scowled. "You should have killed him. He didn't deserve anything better." His face was as hard as granite when he looked up at Troy. "Are you getting chicken-hearted? Think what they did to us Willoubys. Don't let any of them get away."

CHAPTER 10

THROUGH THE WEEK THERE WAS NO WORD TO TELL Mary Barstow if Mike's name had been dropped from Troy's list. Finally when the pressure created by her impatience threatened to wreck her nerves, she saddled her black and rode into town. Her Aunt Lucy Abitz would have the news if there was any to be had.

Lucy was at the water bucket getting a drink when Mary appeared at the kitchen door behind the Abitz store. She called a greeting as she turned to waddle towards her rocker, and Mary went inside, carefully closing the screen door behind her.

"This summer is going to be a hot one if this is a sample," Lucy wheezed, dropping heavily into her chair. "I'm mighty glad you came, Mary. Haven't had anyone to talk to for half a day. Too hot for people to venture out, I guess. Ain't even anybody loafing in the store."

"Nothing much happening to talk about, is there, Aunt Lucy?" Mary asked, opening the way for the gossip to flow.

Lucy threw up her hands in exasperation. "Nothing happening?" she exclaimed. "Everything's been happening. Ed Swazey pulled stakes this past week. The story is that he had a run-in with young Willouby and got told he had just so long to move out. Leastwise he tossed his gear on his old nag and hit for tall timber without so much as saying goodbye. That's another one Willouby can scratch off his list."

"You've heard about his list, too?"

"Huh! Heard about it? There isn't a man, woman, or child between Jericho and Queen City who hasn't heard about it. With the exception of Mike, there ain't a man on that list that's worth two whoops in a rain barrel, and I don't care what Willouby does to them."

"Do you know what Troy's doing? We haven't heard any news all week."

"You mean you haven't heard what's going on? Bless you, child. Sit down there and let me catch a good breath."

Mary settled herself and waited. Aunt Lucy needed no further prompting.

"First off," Lucy began, "if you're wondering about Troy, I can tell you what he was doing a couple of nights ago. There's a new man who comes through town every few days. His name is Henderson. Works for a new mining company up in the Jericho Hills. Seems to be looking for men to hire or something like that. Anyhow, he got into a game at the King's Palace the other night, and things were going wrong for him. Sel was there at the Palace like he is every night. He was watching the game, and he says he's as sure as Henderson was that he was being cheated. But Sel couldn't see how it was being done."

"What does this man Henderson have to do with Troy?" Mary interrupted impatiently.

"Just hold your horses and you'll find out. Henderson had been playing quite a while. He'd lost some, too. He jumped up all of a sudden and called the dealer—that was Ace Belling—and it looked like a gunfight coming up. Everybody scooted for cover, and right then was when Troy stepped in. It would have been curtains sure for Henderson. Belling is a flash with his shoulder derringer. But young Willouby popped up and caught everybody by surprise, and before they knew what was up, he'd shot out every light in the place. By the time somebody got a light going again, Willouby was gone and so was Henderson."

"Wonder why he risked his life to save that mining man?" Mary asked, puzzled.

Lucy shrugged. "No telling. Probably just taking the part of the underdog. Likely he'd been standing out in the shadows watching for some of the men he's gunning for when the ruckus started. At any rate, he was quick enough to outsmart and outshoot that whole room full of hombres, and some of them claim to be real kingpins with a six-gun."

"I don't suppose Henderson will go back to the King's Palace," Mary said, filling a gap as Lucy caught her breath.

"Don't you think it! He'll go back, all right. He's got quite a crush on that singer, Kate Brent. I reckon that helped stir up bad blood between him and Belling. Kate belongs to the working staff there at the Palace same as Ace, and Ace probably figures they're a little above such scum as mining men."

"Has Troy been back in town since?"

"Haven't seen him. The sheriff's red hot on his trail now. He's added the charge of shooting up the Palace and he's out to get him, come flood or famine. He'd better get him, too, if he expects to live much longer. His name is on that list, you know. And Belling's just as keen to get him as the sheriff."

"What's Belling got against Troy?" Mary asked, beginning to get an inkling of what it might be.

"It's the story our noble sheriff is telling. I don't like to repeat it, but you ought to know. He's spreading a tale about you meeting Troy Willouby in the cottonwoods west of your place."

A wave of cold apprehension swept over Mary. "How

64

did he hear anything like that?" she asked, her voice suddenly sinking to a whisper.

"I don't know. But I've got my ideas. Bright and early one morning about a week ago, Ed Swazey rode into town. He talked quite a while to Emitt; then he rode out. Nobody's heard of him since. I figure he told Emitt something, 'cause the sheriff started spreading that tale right away. He's making it sound pretty colorful, too."

The hot blood swept up into Mary's face. "I did meet Troy and I got him to promise not to start trouble with Dad. But that's all there was to it."

"Sakes alive!" Lucy exclaimed. "I'm not doubting you. Don't get so excited. I'm just telling you what's being said. Did you say you got Willouby to promise not to start anything with Mike?"

Mary nodded. "And I think he'll keep that promise. But I don't know what Dad will do if he runs into him."

"Go for a gun if he's got a chance. He knows Troy Willouby's killer reputation. And he'll go gunning for somebody sure when he hears the story Emitt's telling."

"Why did Emitt say that?" Tears fringed Mary's voice. "Why?"

"If you're asking me, I'd say it was jealousy," Lucy said wisely.

"Jealousy?" Mary repeated, trying to fathom Aunt Lucy's reasoning.

"That's what I said. Emitt has always bragged of himself as a great gunslinger. But Willouby has made a monkey of him twice since he came back to the valley. You and I probably have never hated anything enough to be able to understand how much Emitt hates young Willouby. He's jealous of the way Willouby can outwit him. I'm guessing that Swazey saw you and Troy in the cottonwoods the other night and told

65

Emitt. The sheriff grabbed at the chance to hit back at Willouby without having to risk a gunfight. Then, too, if he can get people to believe that story, they'll back him in his efforts to do away with Willouby."

"But it isn't just Troy he's giving a black name."

"Sure it isn't. Your name is getting dragged down worse than Troy's. But Emitt doesn't care about that. He doesn't care how much damage he does to anybody as long as it helps him a little."

Mary looked out the door, her fists clenched into hard knots. "I could almost kill him," she said.

"If I was a man, I would kill him," Lucy said vehemently. "But Sel won't do a thing. Says he can't afford to take sides in this. It would hurt his business. Sometimes I believe he thinks more of his store than he does of me."

"It isn't Uncle Sel's fight," Mary said, gaining control of herself. "It was my fault. I shouldn't have met Troy out there. But I thought I could help Dad."

Lucy reached over and patted Mary's knee. "Don't fret about it, honey. We all make mistakes. And maybe it wasn't a mistake, if you got Troy to lay off Mike. As for Emitt, when a man sinks low enough to start a story like that, he's just about at the end of his string."

Mary tried to take consolation from her aunt's words. But suddenly she felt as if she couldn't stand it in the room another minute. After saying a hurried goodbye, she ran outside. Whipping the knot out of her reins, she mounted and sent the black racing down the street towards the open prairie.

CHAPTER 11

IT WAS LATE THAT NIGHT WHEN MARY HEARD BUDDY come home and climb the ladder to his bed in the attic. He had been staying out later and later, and Mike's remonstrations had no effect on the boy. Mary could have spent long hours worrying about her brother had it not been for so many other things pressing her.

At breakfast, for the first time that Mary could remember, Buddy was too excited to eat. Mary saw Mike studying his son's face. But there were no questions asked. With the meal about over, Buddy could suppress his news no longer.

"I'm going to join the posse today," he said dramatically.

Mike's brows lowered. "Emitt's posse?"

"Sure," Buddy said importantly. "Who else would be swearing in deputies?"

"You're not going with Emitt," Mike said flatly.

"Why not?" Buddy demanded defiantly. "We're going after Troy Willouby. Emitt says he's got to be rounded up for the safety of everybody in the valley. And that includes you, you know."

"Emitt's just as bad as Willouby."

Buddy bristled. "Emitt's a good sheriff. Ace says so."

"Is Ace going in the posse?" Mary asked quickly.

"Naw. He's got his business there in the King's Palace to look after. Emitt's swearing in three or four boys who are in town now looking for work. Ace says it will be good experience for me, besides helping Dad getting rid of Willouby."

"You're pretty light in the saddle for such work," Mike said.

"I can handle a gun with the best of them," Buddy said proudly. "We're meeting this morning and getting our packs set; we'll be out two or three days if we have to. We're not coming back without him."

"Where do you expect to find him?" Mary asked.

"We ain't got any idea where we'll find him," Buddy admitted. "But we'll find him. Don't worry about that."

But Mary did worry.

Time wore on, and when the second night passed with no word from the posse, Mary felt that her nerves had reached the breaking point. Breakfast was a silent affair, tension spreading a blanket over the room, dulling appetites and tightening nerves.

The tension snapped suddenly shortly after noon when a horse trotted into the yard. Mary was the first to reach the window. Her cry of joy brought Mike and Mrs. Barstow crowding around her. Buddy, with all the importance of a sixteen-year-old in command of a situation, dismounted and marched up the path to the house.

"Did you get him?" Mike demanded as Buddy came through the door.

"We had a tough chase," Buddy said, flopping down in a chair and surveying his sister and parents with solemn gaze.

"Probably so," Mike agreed. "But did you get him?"

"No posse ever tackled a tougher job in Storm Valley," Buddy said evasively.

Mary knew her brother's love of dramatics and settled down in a chair to listen. Now that he was the center of attraction, he would take his time before yielding his high position. Mike flopped into a chair at the table, his brows knit together in a dark frown.

"All right," he growled. "Tell it in your own way.

But, hang you, tell it!"

Buddy ignored Mike's outburst, looking calmly over his audience. Only his flashing eyes told of his excitement. "There were only five of us in the posse—me and Emitt and three toughs he'd picked up in town. We didn't find a trace of Willouby the first day out. We were half-way to Jericho when we camped. Yesterday we circled around close to Hermit Peak. Emitt was working on the idea that Willouby must be holed up somewhere in the hills around the valley."

"We ain't interested in your ride over the country," Mike said irritably. "If you didn't find him, say so and be done with it."

Buddy frowned. "We found him, all right. But not over by Hermit Peak. We crossed the creek there and came down along the front of Storm Range. We were over by the big rock almost straight south of here when Emitt located tracks."

A shiver trickled down Mary's spine.

"Just when we were examining the tracks, a horse broke cover from the trees up ahead and started down the valley. We all recognized Willouby's blue roan. We didn't take long getting on his tail. But that roan is the fastest thing that ever hit this valley. It was all we could do to keep him in sight. He didn't seem to be trying to hide from us. He was just leading us down the valley. We never would have caught him, if the roan hadn't started to limp."

Mike's eyes brightened. "You got him cornered then?"

Buddy nodded. "It was almost dark last night when we found his horse. That was about fifteen miles from here on the road to Queen City. He'd been far enough ahead of us to pick out a honey of a place to make a stand. There was a long sloping rock wall he had crawled up; he was crouching on a rock ledge where we couldn't see him from below."

"Did you get him last night?" Mike prodded impatiently.

"We did some shooting last night," Buddy admitted. "But it was pretty dark, and all we wanted to do was to make sure he was up there. We finally got him to take a shot at us. Dark as it was, he grazed one of the boys. You can bet we didn't show ourselves after that shot. Emitt stationed us around so that we could watch every inch of that rock where he could come down. We were all set to pick him off if he tried getting away in the dark."

"Did you have a place to guard?"

Buddy nodded, but there was a scowl on his face. "I had the outside edge where he was least likely to come. Emitt thought I wasn't man enough to stop him if he did come. But I'd have shown him. I had the horses to watch, too. We didn't unsaddle; only loosened the cinches. We wanted to be ready to leave in a hurry just in case Troy slipped past us. We didn't hear a thing from him till this morning. When it got light, the posse hunted cover up close to the wall and started shooting. He shot back, and it got mighty uncomfortable down there."

"Were you in the fight?" Mrs. Barstow asked.

Buddy frowned again. "Naw. Emitt made me hold the horses back to one side. But I could see everything that went on better than if I'd been up close. Sometimes I saw Troy moving around up on the ledge, and once Emitt must have seen him. He really opened up. I saw Troy fall back as if he'd been hit, and there was no more shooting up there."

Mary felt as if a teetering rock had finally fallen on her.

"When they couldn't stir up any more shooting from above, Emitt made one of the men move out a little way while the others covered him. But even a target like that didn't draw any shots. So finally Emitt decided that Troy was dead or hurt so bad he couldn't shoot. He and the three other men fanned out across the rock and started climbing up slow to make sure they'd gotten him."

"You didn't go?" Mike asked.

Buddy's fists balled. "Emitt wouldn't let me. Said I had to watch the horses. They got about half-way up, crawling on hands and knees, everyone keeping a gun in one hand, when I saw Troy again. He stepped out on the ledge, standing up straight, but I could see there was blood on his left arm. He yelled at Emitt, and his gun swung around. Emitt's men didn't move. 'This is between you and me, Emitt,' he said. Emitt looked up, but he didn't do anything else. 'Get him, men!' he yelled, but he didn't try it himself, and nobody else budged. 'Stay out of it,' Troy warned the others. 'Emitt, I ought to kill you for being in that raid years ago. But I'm not going to do it. I'm going to kill you for something else!, Buddy turned to Mary. "Mary, you ought to like this."

"Why should I?" she asked, her voice an unsteady whisper.

"Just listen and you'll see. Troy glared down at Emitt, and I could almost see the hate in his face. 'You've been telling lies about Mary Barstow,' Troy yelled savagely, 'dragging her name in the mud. I'm going to kill you for that, Emitt.' He waited, and nobody moved. I could hear

71

Emitt whimpering as if he was bawling. Finally Troy said, 'I'm waiting!' Emitt reared up then, taking a wild shot at Troy. Troy didn't shoot till Emitt was ready to fire again. Then his gun roared twice, and Emitt folded up like a jack-knife and bounced to the bottom of the wall. Troy swung his gun on the other three, but they let go of their guns and raised their hands. 'Get out of here,' Troy ordered, and they came down pronto.

"I had left the horses tied to some trees behind me," Buddy went on. "When Emitt's men got down, they beat it for the horses and vamoosed. I guess I must have been a little excited. By the time I thought of running, Troy was nearly at the bottom of the slope. I thought that since I was a Barstow, I'd better not let him see me, so I hid. But he came right towards me. I had my gun trained on him and I could have killed him, but I didn't shoot."

"Why?" Mike demanded. "He'd killed the sheriff."

"But you should have seen the way he stood up there on that ledge and called Emitt," Buddy said. "And he gave Emitt more than a fair chance, even though Emitt had been trying to gun him down any way he could. And then he shot Emitt because of what he'd said about Mary. I just couldn't kill him."

Mike nodded and lowered his big head. Mary, looking at her brother, saw a new light in his eyes. It was hero worship such as not even Ace Belling had roused.

"Did Troy see you?" Mary asked.

Buddy nodded. "He saw me and stood facing my gun without blinking. He told me to put up my gun; then he said, 'You're a Barstow, aren't you?' I figured then my goose was cooked. But he only grinned at the way I was shaking and told me to ride to town and tell somebody

72

to come after Emitt. Then he said, 'After this, don't go riding in bad company.' He took Emitt's horse and rode back to where his own roan was grazing. Then he changed horses and rode off. I came by town and told what had happened."

Mary watched her father as he got up and walked to the window to stare blindly at the distant peaks of Storm Range. Suddenly she saw him stiffen. Then he whirled to face her. "Mary," he said sharply, "go to your room."

Mary came to her feet. Mike hadn't spoken to her like that for ten years. "Why, Dad, what's wrong?"

Then she got a glimpse out the window. She saw Ace Belling riding up, immaculately dressed, sitting his saddle importantly as if he owned the world. One look at her father's stern face told her that argument was useless. Turning, she hurried into her room, leaving the door slightly ajar.

She heard Ace's smooth soft-voiced greeting and Mike's brusque reply. Then there were footsteps leading into Mike's office just across from her room. The office door swung shut but failed to latch, leaving a crack an inch wide. That was enough so that Mary, sitting perfectly quiet, could hear everything being said across the hall.

"What did you come out for?" Mike demanded roughly.

"Just calling on Mary," Ace said easily. "But if you have some business to discuss, it can come first."

"It's going to come first. I heard what you've been telling in town—that Mary is your girl. Let me tell you she's not."

Ace's voice lower lowered, and Mary couldn't miss the sinister threat in it. "Don't be in a hurry, Mike. Remember what will happen to you if Mary backs out on me."

"I know what you can do to me," Mike said heavily. "But that doesn't make any difference. That order stands."

"Do you want your neck stretched?"

"I'd rather have that than have you get Mary."

A great exultation swept over Mary. Her faith in Mike was completely vindicated now. But hard on the heels of that first wave of triumph came an icy-fingered, paralyzing fear. Ace still held the whip hand. And he would use his power to destroy Mike. She didn't doubt that.

"What's got into you, Mike?" Ace's voice was soft again.

"I've jumped every time you've snapped your fingers for twelve years, Ace. And I reckon I'd go on jumping if it was just me that was going to suffer. But when you start dragging in my family, I draw the line."

"That's a nice speech, Mike. Too bad your family can't hear it. You're making a mistake. And I'm gambling you'll realize it when you think it over. I'm giving you twenty-four hours to change your mind."

"The answer will be the same." Mike's voice was sharp with determination, "twenty-four hours from now or twenty-four years. Don't go near Mary again. She's not your girl and she never will be as long as I'm alive."

With a curse, Ace kicked a chair out of his path on the way to the door. "It's no fun to be hanged, Mike. Think about it. I'll give you twenty-four hours. Either you change your mind or I'll change it for you."

Mary heard Mike's heavy steps charging towards the office door and Ace's light quick steps retreating through the kitchen. She sat motionless, all the exultation gone from her. Ace Belling had become as

74

great a threat to the peace of the Barstow household as Troy Willouby had ever been.

CHAPTER 12

DARKNESS HAD MANTLED THE VALLEY FOR ALMOST AN hour when Troy dismounted in the cottonwoods. He led the horse to the edge of the grove nearest the Barstow house and tied him. Then he walked quickly to the kitchen door and knocked. Mary opened the door, then stepped back, stifling a gasp.

"Evening, Mary," Troy said politely, smothering the turmoil that broke loose inside him.

"What do you want?" she asked, her voice a low whisper. "Go away. Please."

Troy shook his head. "I came to see your father." He saw alarm flash over her face and added, "There's nothing to be afraid of. I made a promise, remember?"

"Then why do you want to see Dad?"

"I figure it's time we got a look at each other."

Reluctantly, Mary moved back and motioned him inside. He stepped in, hat in hand, and followed her into the next room. Mike was seated in a chair at the far side of the room, and Troy instantly remembered the wedge-shaped face and heavy eyebrows. But except for those characteristics, he wouldn't have recognized the man.

Mike stared at the visitor for a moment, then came from his chair, realization of his identity sweeping over him. "What do you want, Willouby?"

"Just a chance to meet you face to face, Barstow, and see what kind of a jellyfish you are. You've managed to dodge me ever since I came back."

"I've been in town every day, but I haven't seen you

75

loafing around."

Troy studied Barstow's face. Worry stood out sharply on his features, the strain of it cutting deep lines about his mouth and eyes. But the two things he looked for most were missing. Hate and fear were in neither his face nor his bearing. The leader of that fateful raid should hate the man who had come back to avenge those who had died. And he should fear the avenger unless he was certain of victory over him. And Barstow could hardly be sure of that now.

Uncertainty gripped Troy. This was not the kind of man he had trained himself to hate over the last eight years. Barstow was watching him silently, intently.

"How come you sent your boy in the posse after me instead of coming yourself?" Troy asked deliberately.

"I didn't send him. I wouldn't have sent a dog with Emitt."

There was hate in Barstow's voice now, but it was not directed at Troy. Troy understood how Barstow might hate Emitt. And for an instant there was a common ground between him and Barstow. Quickly he spun towards the door. This was not as it should be. The longer he stayed in this room, the more he felt a traitor to his father.

Mary overtook him as he reached the outside door. She caught his sleeve and he turned, half-way through the door.

"You'll keep your promise, won't you?" Her voice was a whisper.

"I'll keep it," he said.

Whirling back, he crossed the yard in rapid strides, reaching his horse before turning. Mary was still in the doorway, but even as he looked she stepped back, shutting the door and cutting off the square of light streaming into the yard.

Slowly Troy mounted and reined into the cotton-woods.

He was half-way through the cottonwood grove when he suddenly jerked to a halt as a shot shattered the night over close to the barn. Without hesitation, he wheeled his roan in that direction. Nearing the barn, which stood at the edge of the grove, he slid out of the saddle and ran forward, his gun in the clear. It was then he caught the drumming of hoofbeats on the road to town.

The late moon had not yet come up, and the thin light from the stars was almost useless in the shade of the big trees. A groan close by the barn door was the first sign of life that he heard. Moving forward, he found Buddy slumped against the side of the barn, gripping a bleeding shoulder and swaying back and forth, mumbling incoherently. He knelt beside the boy and examined the wound, a clean bullet hole going through the muscle under the shoulder.

"Come on, son," Troy said gently. "You've got to get to the house."

But Buddy only rocked back and forth, moaning softly. Troy realized then that the shock had jarred the boy's senses. Stooping, he picked him up and started towards the house. The door of the house was open, and Mike Barstow was just coming through with a lighted lantern. When Troy came into the circle of light thrown by the lantern, Mike came to an abrupt halt.

"Get a place ready to put him," Troy said sharply. "I don't think he's hurt bad."

Mary and her mother moved quickly ahead of Troy, and the cot in one corner of the living-room was waiting by the time he got to it. Laying the boy down gently, he turned to face the three watching him.

77

It was only then that he saw the suspicion in their faces. Something that was rapidly building into hate twisted Mike's face.

"You didn't have nerve enough to shoot me, so you tried to kill my boy." A growing fury sharpened Barstow's voice. "Is that the kind of a fighter you are?"

Troy went tight inside. "I didn't shoot the kid. I found him out by the barn after somebody else shot him."

Barstow's eyes were wild now, and his hand began inching across his chest above the gun he had jammed into his waistband before running out to investigate the shot.

Troy tensed, his eyes boring into the rancher. "Careful, Barstow," he snapped. "Don't start something you can't finish. Let the kid talk. Do you think I'd have brought him in if I'd shot him?"

But Barstow, breathing hard as if from a long run, kept his hand moving, his eyes blazing with hatred of Troy. Troy waited, knowing what he would have to do in another instant, looking for some way to avoid it and seeing none. Then, as Mike's hand shaped into a claw ready to grab the gun, Mary screamed and threw herself forward, grasping Mike's hand.

"Don't!" she cried. "Wait till you're sure. Buddy will tell."

For an instant Mike struggled with Mary; then he stopped, his shoulders sagging, a beaten, weary man, the tension draining out of his face. He slumped into a chair as Mary took the gun from him and shoved it to the back of the table. Troy turned back to the cot.

"Got any hot water?" he asked, tearing away the shirt from the wound.

With Mary's help and bandages and hot water brought by Mrs. Barstow, Troy soon had the wound

78

dressed. Eventually Buddy began taking notice of the proceedings.

"How do you feel, son?" Troy asked.

"Kinda sick," Buddy said weakly. "But I'll be all right." He looked around the room at Mary, then at Troy. "What are you doing here?"

Mary answered, "He brought you here after you were shot."

Troy caught Mary's hesitation and knew that doubt was gripping her, too. He turned towards the door.

"I'll get the doc," he said.

"Just a minute," Mike said ominously, showing new life as he moved towards the cot. "Do you feel like talking, Bud?"

The boy nodded. The color was slowly coming back to his face. "I'm all right, Dad."

"Who shot you?"

Troy saw the tenseness in the faces of Mike and his daughter as they leaned over the cot to catch the answer. There was no hesitation in Buddy's reply.

"I don't know. I didn't know anybody was near when I rode up to the barn. Then just as I started to get off my horse, somebody fired. I fell pretty hard, but I didn't pass out right away."

"Did you see who it was?" The question came from Mike, and his voice was hoarse and ragged.

Buddy shook his head. "No. Somebody rode out of the shadow of the trees and leaned over me, but I couldn't see who it was. He said, 'Tell your old man this is just a warning. It will be worse next time.' After that I don't remember what happened till I came to in here."

Mary was looking at Troy, her eyes big. "It was you, Troy!" she exclaimed bitterly, her voice barely more than a whisper.

"No, it wasn't Troy," Buddy said quickly. "I could see well enough to tell it was a little man. Troy ain't little."

For no reason that Troy could see, Mary smiled then. She turned back to her brother, and Mike twisted slowly to face Troy. A shock ran over Troy as he saw him. Ten years had suddenly piled on the man's shoulders. The lines at his eyes and mouth were deep gashes in a gray face, and his eyes were wide and almost glassy.

"I'm sorry I accused you, Willouby," he said in a toneless voice. "I know now who shot Bud. Get the doc, please."

"Sure." Troy turned and left the house.

CHAPTER 13

THE SECOND DAY AFTER HIS VISIT TO THE BARSTOW ranch, Troy brought supplies from town. Boone was posted at the look-out. Troy was almost to the cave when he heard a shot. He dumped the supplies at Dan's feet in front of the cave and urged his horse up the narrow trail.

He found Boone at the look-out, rifle held shakily in his hand. Sweat stood out on his forehead, and his tightly pressed lips were a white slit across his face.

"What happened?" Troy demanded.

"I just shot a man," Boone said, his voice thick.

"Who? Where is he?"

Boone pointed down the dim trail towards the big rock. "He's down there. I don't know who he is."

"Why did you shoot him?"

"He was coming up. I figured he'd found us. I got scared, I guess."

Troy tied the roan and started down the trail. "Come on. We've got to see who it is."

Boone hesitated. "I don't think I killed him."

Caution stopped Troy. "How far down is he?"

"A couple of hundred yards, anyway."

Troy moved down the slope, his gun in his hand. It might be that the man was only wounded and still full of fight.

His speed slackened as he dropped lower. Then he caught a glimpse of a man lying beside a rock a few yards ahead. He moved, and Troy gripped his gun tighter.

"Take it easy, mister. I've got you covered like a blanket."

The man beside the rock became motionless as Troy moved closer. Then, ten feet away, Troy recognized him. He ran forward, the gun in his hand almost forgotten.

"Are you hit bad, Barstow?" he asked, dropping on one knee.

Mike Barstow shook his head. "I don't think so. But I wasn't going to show myself and draw another slug. This one's in my shoulder."

Quickly Troy examined it. "Not so bad," he said. "But it's still in there. That will be a job for the doc. Sorry about this. Boone got excited, I guess. Nobody had found this trail before."

"I wouldn't have found it if Mary hadn't told me about it."

"How did she know?"

"She guessed that you were holed up in a cave up there somewhere. She said this trail would take me

81

there. I wanted to see you or your dad and do something that should have been done when you first came back. Only then I didn't have nerve enough to do it."

Boone arrived then, still gripping his rifle. "Here, give me a hand," Troy commanded. "We'll get him up under that ledge and make him as comfortable as we can while I ride to town for the doc."

Leaning on the two Willoubys, Mike climbed the steep slope. Troy broke off some small pine limbs to make a blanket for the hard rock under the ledge. There Mike was settled out of the sun and made as comfortable as possible. Then Troy turned to get his horse. But Mike stopped him.

"The doc can wait a little. I came up here to tell you something I should have told you long ago. I want to do it now."

Troy sensed the urgency driving the man, so he hunched down against a boulder to listen.

"I worked on a railroad back in Ohio before I came west," Mike began. "Things were pretty tough for me and my family. A kid came along one day and made me an offer. I knew he was on the wrong side of the law, but there didn't seem to be any chance of a slip-up in the proposition he outlined, and I needed money. There was a box of fancy jewels going to be shipped through before long, and they were to come to the town where I lived. Working where I did I would know when they came. The kid and I were going to steal the jewels, and my half would put me on easy street.

"The jewels came, all right. Got in town about ten at night. There wasn't anybody there to get them off the train as we expected. I suppose, since the shipment was secret, they thought they were safe. The kid sent me into the express depot to make the guard open the safe where

82

they were put. I got inside without causing any alarm because the guard knew me. But he put up a fight. I killed him. It was the only time I ever shot a man."

Barstow's voice broke.

"I got away and met this kid outside of town," he went on after a minute. "I had the jewel box. But when we opened it there was nothing but paper and rocks inside. It looked like somebody else had already taken the jewels and substituted this other stuff. I knew the police would be hot after the killer of the guard, so I got my family and moved west. I took a homestead in eastern Nebraska. It was way off the beaten track. We didn't have any close neighbors. I thought we'd be safe there.

"But one afternoon this kid and a couple of strangers rode in. They stayed all night. The kid told me the police were hot on my trail, and if I didn't want him to turn me in, I'd better do what he said. I've been kowtowing to him ever since."

"Who is this kid?" Troy asked. "Anybody I know?"

Barstow nodded. "You know him, all right. It's Ace Belling. He told me I had to move here to this valley. So the next day I told my family the visitors had described a garden of Eden to me and we were moving there. When we got here, Ace made me start riding your dad every time I met him. He said he wanted the ranch you Willoubys were on."

"Did he give any reason for wanting it?" Things were beginning to drop into place for Troy now.

"Sure, he gave a reason. Said the railroad was going to build through this valley, and the right-of-way would go through the land you held. He wanted it to sell to the railroad. I hated myself every time I jumped on your dad, but I didn't have any choice."

Troy nodded grimly. "Then you were on the raid when they killed Mother and my sister and brother?"

"No," Mike said emphatically. "Ace sent me to Queen City that afternoon for some supplies he wanted. I heard about the raid when I got home, and I knew I'd be blamed by the Willoubys and everybody else. But there wasn't a thing I could do. If I so much as said a word, Ace would have turned me over to the law. After you'd been gone two or three years, they put up your ranch for sale and made me bid for it. Didn't cost much. I figured the only reason they wanted me on it was to make sure you'd go after me and let them alone if you did come back."

Troy was watching Barstow closely. And he knew he was hearing the truth. "They had it figured about right."

"Anyway, since you came back, Ace has been trying to get me out of the country."

"Then Ace Belling is the leader of the raiders?" Troy asked, certain of his answer now.

But Barstow shook his head. "I don't think so. I've been sure ever since I got here that Ace was getting his orders from someone. And after thinking about it, I'm certain he was acting on orders when he talked me into working with him on that robbery back in Ohio. But I don't know who gives the orders."

"Why is he trying to get rid of you now?"

"I've got a hunch he thinks I know something I don't. He's afraid I'll talk and get him into more trouble than he can handle."

Troy rubbed his chin thoughtfully. "Maybe you have. I've got a score to settle with him now."

"There's something else. I'm sure of it. It doesn't make sense that they'd kill just to get a right-of-way to sell to the railroad. Besides, I haven't heard anything more about a railroad. Anyway, when he tried to make me turn Mary over to him, I balked. I'm not much of a man, but I haven't sunk low enough to stand by and let him get his hands on Mary. He said he'd make me change my mind. He shot Bud the other night as the first step."

"It takes a coward to do a thing like that," Troy said, his distrust of Belling crystallizing into a cold hate.

Barstow shook his head. "He's not a coward. He's a killer. He'll do anything to get what he wants. This trick of his didn't work, though. I sent Bud and his mother out on the stage this morning. Mary and I are going as soon as I get things straightened out with you Willoubys."

"There isn't much to straighten out now," Troy said. "We've caused you a lot of grief lately, accusing you of leading that raid on us."

"I ain't blaming you for that. Ace had it fixed so you couldn't think anything else. But there's something I came here to do." He fished through his pocket with his good hand. "Here," he said, bringing out a paper. "This is the deed to that ranch. I got it when I bid it in at the sheriff's sale. It's yours. It should never have been anybody else's."

Troy took it, watching the glow on Mike Barstow's face.

"What will you do when you leave this valley?" Troy asked slowly.

"I'll hang, I suppose," Barstow said heavily. "But it's no worse to face the noose than to have it dangling over your head where you can't see it."

"Does Mary know what you did back in Ohio?"

Mike's eyes dropped. "Nobody knows but Ace and those he's told. I couldn't bring myself to tell my family. They're everything I've lived for. They respect me. I wish they'd never have to know."

Troy nodded, sympathy for the man rising in him. He rose and turned towards his horse.

"I'll go for the doc, and he'll get that slug picked out. I'd better bring Mary back with me."

"I wish you would," Barstow said. "I don't like her being there alone."

Troy got his horse, then turned to his brother. "See that Barstow is as comfortable as you can make him; then you'd better get back down to the cave and tell Dad what the ruckus was about. He'll get pretty upset. You'll be all right alone, I guess, Barstow."

"Sure I will," Mike said. But as he started down the trail Troy could see the pain twisting Mike's face.

CHAPTER 14

THERE WAS NO MOVEMENT AROUND THE BARSTOW ranch house as Troy passed it on the way to town. He had decided it was best to wait until he had got the doctor before stopping to explain the situation to Mary. That wasn't going to be an easy task. But still there was a lift to Troy's spirits as he thought of seeing Mary again. There would be a difference now. No longer would he have to cling to his resolve to ruin Mike Barstow. The barrier that had stood so formidably between them was gone.

Riding into town, his eyes traveled over the front of the King's Palace. Ace Belling was probably there. And now Troy had placed Ace in Mike Barstow's place at the head of the list of raiders.

Troy didn't find it hard to picture Ace Belling as a man who could lead a raid such as the one against the Willoubys. Nor would he have much difficulty in turning his hatred on the man.

He pushed on towards the doctor's office. The hour of reckoning would come, but this was not it. The doctor was in his office, just back from the hotel where he had eaten his dinner. At sight of Troy, he reached for his hat and his satchel.

"Who's shot now?" he demanded.

"Mike Barstow. Got a bullet in his shoulder. Bring some thing to dig it out."

"I've always got something for jobs like that. Where is he ?"

"Up at the look-out above the cave. Let's go."

"I thought you could shoot straighter than that," Holmes said as he stepped through the office door.

"I didn't do this. My brother did."

When they got to the cottonwoods at Barstow's, Troy reined up. "At the big rock, turn to your right," he directed. "You'll find a dim trail that leads right up to the look-out. Barstow is there."

"Aren't you going with me?"

"Not now. I've got to explain things to Mary. I'll be along pretty soon."

The doctor grinned. "Hate to stop, don't you?"

Troy found the grin contagious. "Maybe." He reined off the trail while the doctor splashed into the ford.

Troy pulled up in front of the Barstow house and dismounted. His heart was thumping entirely too fast, creating pressure on his chest. Another minute and he would see Mary. This was his first close look at the front of the house in daylight. The flowers that he had noticed there when riding along the trail were blooming brighter now; the early blooms were gone, but the summer's blossoms were in full glory.

Regret twisted a knife in him. This might have been the way his mother and sister would have kept the yard if they had lived. Troy had not had anything like this to call home since he had left the valley. His had been a hard man's world; his lessons had been learned in the bitter school of hate and vengeance. Things of beauty such as this yard had had no place in his life, and now it struck a strange chord in him. With a shock he realized he had been missing a big part of life, a soft, kind side of living that he had barely realized existed.

The door opened then and Mary stood there, dressed in levis and a heavy shirt.

"If you're looking for Dad," she said, "he's not here now."

Troy caught the frigidness in her tone, and behind it a note of uneasiness.

"I know where he is," Troy said, stopping a few feet from the door. "He's been hurt, and I came to take you to him."

Her hand flew to her throat. "Hurt? How bad?"

"Not bad," Troy said hastily. "Just a little wound. the doc is fixing him up. He didn't want to leave you here alone."

"Where is he?"

"Up at the look-out above the rock south of here."

Suspicion came into her eyes. "He was going up to see you. You shot him."

"Boone did," Troy corrected her. "He thought it was somebody looking for trouble."

"Can Dad come home tonight?"

"Probably. But you'd better go prepared to stay over just in case the doc says it's better for him to wait till tomorrow."

Mary disappeared into the house. Troy tied his horse and went to the barn. Mary's black stood there, and he saddled and bridled him. When he led the horse back, Mary was waiting, a small bundle under her arm.

"Did Dad talk to you?" she asked.

"He talked a lot. I know now that he wasn't on that raid."

Her face brightened. "I'm glad," she said, a catch in her voice. "Now let's go. I want to see him."

They splashed across the ford and took the trail at a long lope. Exultation swept over Troy as he rode beside the girl. It would be a new world for them now. Their differences had vanished. And he realized that those differences had all been of his making.

While she rode facing straight ahead, he let his eyes stray to her. Her hair was slipping free of its pins and working out from under her hat; the golden strands glistened in the sun. She sat straight in the saddle with an easy grace that comes only from long hours of riding.

And suddenly he thought of Mike's statement that he and Mary were going east as soon as he had straightened things out with the Willoubys. He was straight with the Willoubys now, so there was nothing to stop them from leaving the valley. Mike would be able to go in a day or two at the outside. And Mary would go with him. The day suddenly lost its brightness for Troy, and the buoyancy in him died.

Then, as they neared the big rock, the sharp snap of a shot echoed down to them. Troy hauled up on his reins, but he was no quicker than Mary.

"Where was that?" she asked, her eyes wide with

apprehension.

"Don't know," Troy lied, trying to calm the misgivings that erupted in him. His eyes searched the sloping wall around the look-out.

Then he caught sight of the doctor's horse, still a couple of hundred yards from the top, lunging up the steep incline. Troy waited and in a moment was rewarded by a glimpse of a horse clambering over the loose rocks and through the trees to the right of the look-out. To the left ran the trail down to the cave.

Troy was certain then. But he said nothing to Mary. Instead, he urged his horse on past the big rock towards the trail up the slope; Mary followed. There could be but one reason that rider had cut out along the face of the wall where the going was so precarious. He didn't want to be seen by anyone on either of the trails. And to Troy the shot could mean only one thing.

He pushed the roan as hard as he dared as he climbed towards the look-out, Mary's horse dropping behind. He saw the doctor kneeling at Mike Barstow's side as he brought his heaving mount to a stop and leaped off. Running forward, he took a look at Barstow's ashen face and the blood on his shirt front and had his answer.

"Pretty bad, is it, Doc?" he asked.

Holmes nodded. "He's still conscious. He wants to talk to you."

Troy knelt beside Barstow. "What is it, Mike? Who shot you?"

Mike opened his eyes. "Ace Belling. Must have followed me today. Waited till you were all gone. Tried to keep me from telling something I didn't know. Must be something important."

Sweat stood out on Mike's forehead. Troy glanced at Holmes. "He shouldn't talk, should he?"

Tight-lipped, Holmes nodded. "Better let him say what he wants to."

Troy turned back to the dying man. "I'll find out what it is, Mike," he said.

"Good." A trace of a grin tugged at the corner of Barstow's mouth. "At least this is better than a rope." His voice weakened. "Don't let Ace get Mary. You take care of her—Troy."

Troy was struck by the irony of it. This morning Mike Barstow had still been at the head of his list of men marked to suffer for the murderous raid on the Willoubys. Now he was being asked by Barstow to look after his daughter.

"Sure, Mike," he said gently. "I'll see that Mary is taken care of."

"Keep her away from Ace," Mike insisted, straining to make his words coherent. "Promise?"

"I promise, Mike," Troy said.

Satisfied, Mike slumped back, and Holmes knelt quickly to feel his pulse.

"How about it?" Troy asked softly.

Holmes waited a minute, then nodded. "That's it."

Troy stood up and turned. Mary stood five feet away, her hands hanging motionless at her sides, her face a pasty white. Her eyes were staring unblinkingly at Troy.

"I was sure of it," she said, and her voice was toneless, "when I heard the shot."

There were no tears in her eyes, and the doctor stepped past Troy to place a steady hand on her arm. "Take it easy, Mary," he said gently.

Troy stood helplessly by while Holmes plucked a tiny bottle from his satchel, uncorked it and waved it under her nose.

"Better get her somewhere where she can lie down.

Take her down to your cave. It isn't far, is it?"

Troy shook his head. "A quarter of a mile."

"That's the best we can do. This is going to be tough. Mike meant a lot to her. And she's your responsibility now."

"But what will I do if she takes this too hard?"

"She'll be all right," Holmes said confidently. "I know her better than you do. She's got a strong constitution. Just get her to the cave where she can lie down, have a long cry and a good sleep. That's what she needs."

Troy took Mary's arm and helped her back on her horse. Sobs were shaking her body now, and Troy resisted an urge to take her in his arms and comfort her. When he had mounted, Troy looked down at Holmes.

"Go ahead," the doctor said. "I'll look after things here."

Taking the reins from Mary's hand, Troy slipped them over the horse's head, then started down the trail, leading the girl's mount. Half-way down, he met Boone and explained the situation to him. Boone, inside the cave, had failed to hear the shot up above.

Hurrying back ahead of Troy, Boone piled blankets on pine boughs, making a soft bed in one of the small pockets off the main room of the cave. Troy lifted the girl, now completely succumbed to her grief, and carried her to the bed. Then, hanging a blanket in front of the opening, he went out to take care of the horses.

True to the doctor's predictions, Mary was master of herself again when morning came. Hollow-cheeked and dark-eyed, she came out from her little den when Dan had breakfast cooking. Troy, just back with a bucket of water from the spring a hundred yards down the slope, watched her move up to the fire and had to admit that even the marks of her grief didn't detract too much from her appeal.

She brightened as the day wore on. Troy's mind turned again and again to the promise he had made to Mike. He was not to let Ace Belling touch Mary. And the only sure way of accomplishing that was to eliminate Ace. He might send him out of the valley as he had Ed Swazey. But Troy doubted if Ace could be bluffed. The only way Ace would leave would be the way Slagg had gone. And Ace posed a different problem from Slagg. Slagg had not been keyed to the point necessary to meet a lightning gunman. But now Troy was a marked man. Ace would be ready. And Ace was faster than Slagg, according to all reports.

Tonight was the time to strike. The sooner Ace was mastered, the surer Troy was of keeping his promise to Mike. Ace was a threat, the kind of a threat that could not be ignored for a single instant. But still Troy hesitated.

In the afternoon Boone rode down the canyon on his way to town. But it was not until the sun was tipping the wall across the canyon from the cave that Troy got a chance to see Mary alone. She had stayed inside the cave with Dan most of the day. Now she came out and leaned against one of the huge pines at the mouth of the cave, watching the last glow of the sun across the canyon. Troy came up beside her, searching for the words to say what he wanted without sounding blunt and heartless.

"You heard what your dad said yesterday didn't you?"

She nodded without looking at him. "He made you responsible for me. But I won't be a burden. I'll catch the stage tomorrow and go back where Mother and

Buddy are."

"No hurry," Troy said quickly, knowing that what she suggested was the proper thing but not wanting to see her go. "Wait till you're feeling better. Traveling is pretty tiring." He paused. "You heard what he said about Ace?"

She nodded. "That you were to keep me away from him? That won't be hard. I'll soon be gone."

"But it was Ace who killed Mike," Troy plunged on. "And it was Ace who led that raid on us Willoubys. You know what that means?"

She turned to him for the first time. "No, Troy," she said softly. "You mustn't go after Ace."

Troy tried to read into her voice concern for Ace Belling, but it wasn't there. Neither could he be certain there was any anxiety for his own safety.

"You know I've got to," he said.

"No," she said again. "There have been too many killings. Another one won't right any of the wrongs already done. Are you doing this for me, Troy, or because of the raid years ago?"

He paused. In an instant he knew the answer. The raid seemed centuries behind him now.

"For you, I guess."

"Then let Ace go. Dad wouldn't want you to take the risk even for me, and revenge won't do him any good now."

He clutched at the first hint that she might be concerned about his safety. "I'm used to taking chances," he said. "And as long as Ace is allowed to go free, nobody is safe. What happened yesterday is proof of that."

She gripped his arm. "Please, Troy. I'd feel I was to blame. I couldn't stand that. Promise me you'll not go

94

after Ace."

Giddiness swept over Troy again.

"I promise," he said, and he was surprised at the huskiness that had crept into his voice.

"Thank you," she said softly.

Troy, watching her, found himself looking deep into blue eyes that seemed almost purple. And there were depths in those eyes that stirred emotions inside him he had not known existed. Her hand still rested on his arm, and her touch was like a fire burning through him.

For a minute he stared at her as she swayed slightly towards him. Then he reached out, bringing her to him. His lips found hers as naturally as flowers seek the sun.

For a long minute he held her, conscious only that she was clinging to him. Then he stepped back, realization of what he had done and how unfair he had been sweeping over him. The instant he released her she dropped back against the pine.

"I'm sorry I did that, Mary," he said shakily. "I had no right. Your dad didn't mean that when he asked me to look after you."

Her eyes were on her feet. "I don't think he would have objected," she said, her voice a muted whisper.

"I didn't mean any disrespect to you, Mary," he said earnestly.

Her eyes came up to meet his. "I'm not sorry," she said softly. Then she slid around the pine and disappeared into the cave.

CHAPTER 15

AT BREAKFAST, WHICH MARY HELPED DAN PREPARE, Troy saw in her eyes that she was remembering the night before. But still he found no regret there. For a moment he allowed himself to believe that it had not been her overwrought condition that had driven her to him. But then he put a curb on his enthusiasm. Only time could provide the irrevocable answer.

Boone hadn't returned the night before, and uneasiness plagued Troy. Boone had stayed in town several nights, and Troy always breathed easier when he rode back to the cave.

When he heard the horse outside an hour after breakfast was finished, relief swept over him and he went out leisurely to meet his brother. But it wasn't Boone on the horse at the cave entrance. It was Dr. Holmes, and he didn't have his satchel. Apprehension caught at Troy. He stepped quickly past the pines to his visitor.

"What's wrong, Doc?" he demanded.

"It's your brother, Boone."

"Dead?" The word came from Troy in a croak.

Holmes shook his head. "No. just a couple of bullet holes. I patched him up."

"Where is he?"

"Back in town."

"Who did it?"

"Ace Belling. But you'd better let Kate tell you. She's waiting for you down by the big rock."

"What did she have to do with it?" Suspicion edged Troy's voice.

"I think I'll let her tell you that, too. I don't know too much about it. Kate's one of these people who knows a lot of things but doesn't tell them unless she has a reason. She didn't have a reason to tell me."

"What makes you think she has a reason to tell me?"

"That's what she came out to do."

96

"Did she see you come up here?"

"Not unless she's pretty clever. I left her sitting in the shade of the big rock while I went the long way around to get here. I think you'll change your mind a little about her after you talk to her. Better come along."

"Sure, Doc."

Troy caught his horse and saddled him, then followed Holmes down the canyon trail to come out in the main valley a half-hour later. A horse was standing by the big rock, and as they rode closer, a woman came around from the shady side.

"Reckon I'll get back to town now," Holmes said as they reined up. "I'm not needed any more."

"That's right," Kate said briskly. "Thanks for bringing him."

Holmes lifted a hand in salute and disappeared behind a cloud of dust. Troy turned to the singer.

"Doc said Boone was hurt."

"He is," Kate said matter-of-factly. "But he'll pull through, all right."

"If he's in town, won't Ace find him and finish what he started?"

Kate laughed shortly. "No chance of Ace finding him. I've got him hidden in the little cellar under the shack where I live. Ace thinks he's either dead or a long way from town. I heard him tell Purdy so this morning."

"Doc said you wanted to tell me something. I'm listening."

"Better get down and rest your saddle. It will take a little while."

Troy dismounted. "Must be something important to bring you out this early."

"You'll think it's important," Kate said sharply. "Boone and I risked our necks to get this information."

97

Troy frowned. "Information for me?"

"Now you're getting smart. Boone and me—well, we're like that." She held up two fingers tight together. "We took a fancy to each other as soon as he started coming into the Palace. He's been posing as Jim Henderson, a miner. But I reckon you know that. He gambled some, but he wouldn't drink. Ace got suspicious of him, then acted sort of jealous when he found out Boone was hanging around to see me. But Ace has no string on me.

"After Boone and I got chummy, Boone told me who he really was and what he wanted to find out to help you. He said you didn't have all the names of the men on that raid. For a while I didn't know where to start looking, but I finally got a lead through friends of Slagg." Troy leaned against the rock, listening intently.

"I suspected Ace, and when Boone came in last night and told me what had happened out here, I knew I was right. After one of my numbers I went back as if to change, but I didn't go to my dressing-room. I headed straight for Purdy's room. I figured I might find something there that would brand Ace as the leader of the raid. I'd been trying for two weeks to get a chance to look through Purdy's office. Last night was the first time I found it empty.

"I leafed through Purdy's books and ransacked his drawers and didn't find a thing. But I've worked for the King a long time, and I knew his weakness for secret drawers. I found one of them, and in it the key to his wall safe. I opened the safe and hit the jackpot. I found his payroll book; it listed the work his men had done for him. In the front part of the book I found he had paid six men for a night raid on Dan Willouby."

Excitement burned through Troy. "Who were the

six?"

"You've guessed some of them. Slagg and Emitt and the Swazeys were four. Ace Belling and Jake Finley were the other two. Finley, by the way, was shot in the leg on that raid. Poison set in and the leg had to come off. Now he's got a wooden stub. Boone said there were seven on the raid, so it's a safe bet Purdy himself was the other one, since he only paid six men. So there are only Purdy, Ace and Finley left. And Boone was telling me that you were asked by a marshal friend of yours to see if you could locate some stolen jewels here in Storm Valley. I think I can tell you about them, too."

"Keep talking," Troy said, excitement coursing through him. "Did this same gang have something to do with the jewels?"

"Part of the gang. I found some other papers and notes that told about some jewels. Two rings and two necklaces, I think it was."

Troy nodded. "Those are the ones."

"Only three of the gang were in on that deal. Seems like it was something special. The other men were just gunnies, used only when there was dirty work to be done."

"What three?" Troy pressed.

"The King, Ace and Jake Finley. They got the jewels years ago. I couldn't find out just when. As far as I could see from the papers I found, they must still have them."

Troy came away from the rock. "Thanks, Kate. I've been beating my head against a stone wall for two months trying to find out the things you've just told me." Suddenly he stopped. In the excitement of learning the facts he'd been trying to unearth, he had forgotten his brother. "How did Boone get hurt in all this mess?"

"I was finding this out for him," Kate said. "When I'd about finished reading the papers in the King's safe, I heard somebody coming. I crammed everything back and slipped out the back door of his office. I went out right away and caught Boone's eye. We had a signal we used when either of us wanted to meet the other one outside. If I hadn't been in such a hurry, nobody would have caught on. But I forgot about my next number. When I didn't come on, Ace got suspicious. Maybe he'd caught on to our signals. Anyway, he bobbed up right when I was telling Boone what I'd found out.

"Boone put up a good scrap. He lunged into Ace before Ace could shoot, and that saved his life. I got into the fight, but Ace broke away and started using his gun. Boone was hit twice, but I couldn't see how bad. I jumped on Ace again, and this time I knocked the gun out of his hand. But I was no match for him. I knew he'd try to kill me next, so I lit out of there fast while he was picking up his gun. He fired a couple of shots at me, but I was too far away and dodging like a rabbit. I thought he'd make sure of Boone, but he must have thought Boone was dead. Anyway, he took after me. But I gave him the slip and circled back to Boone."

"How bad was Boone hit?" Troy asked anxiously.

"Not so bad. One slug in the shoulder and the other in the calf of his leg. I had quite a time getting him to my shack, but I managed it and got the doc there to fix him up. Then this morning Doc brought me out here."

"When can Boone be moved?"

"I don't figure he needs to be moved."

"But he isn't safe in town."

"As long as Ace thinks Boone is dead or gone, he won't look through town. for him. There isn't a safer place in the state. Anyway, he belongs to me. We're

100

going to be married."

A shock ran over Troy. But it passed quickly.

"You have my best wishes, Kate," he said. "When can I see Boone?"

"Any time that you can slip in without being seen. If you're seen coming to my shack, it will be curtains for Boone. Ace is a killer of the worst kind. What are you going to do about him?"

Troy started to answer, then stopped short, thinking of Mary and his promise to her. Now Ace had even more to answer for. But was it enough to cause him to break his promise? "He deserves killing," he said finally.

"You'd better see that he gets it," Kate said. "You're the only one who can. And if you fail, it's going to be tough for a lot of us. Boone will never be able to show his face around here, and even I'll have to be mighty careful. I reckon now Ace knows that you're on to him and his part in that raid, so he'll be rarin' to get you before you get him. And there's something else you ought to know. Boone tells me Mike Barstow put Mary in your care. I've heard Ace say dozens of times he was going to have Mary. Ace doesn't make idle threats. Now that he knows the cat is out of the bag, he's liable to do anything."

Icy fingers touched Troy's spine. Ace had demonstrated his diabolical ability to follow through on his threats by his cold-blooded murder of Mike Barstow. Mary wasn't safe for an instant now. It was her safety, along with the safety of others, against his promise. And deep in his heart Troy knew which must come first.

"I've got my job cut out for me," he said, reaching for his reins. "Thanks for everything you've done, Kate.

Tell Boone I'll take care of things."

He swung into the saddle and rode back the way he had come. When he looked back towards the rock, Kate was on her way to town, leaving a trail of dust.

Mary was at the cave entrance when he reached it. He dismounted and left the reins dangling.

"How is Boone?" Mary asked as he came towards her.

"Kate says he isn't hurt bad. She's taking care of him."

"Who did it?"

"Ace Belling." Troy realized that too much of his feeling had crept into his voice.

Mary was looking at him, her eyes wide and fearful. Then slowly her gaze fell. "I guess I'm to blame," she said, and there was a catch in her voice. "If I hadn't kept you back last night, you might have stopped Ace before he shot Boone."

"I doubt it," Troy said quickly. "Don't blame yourself, Mary. Anyway, thanks to Kate, Boone isn't dead. Ace will kill him, though, if he ever sees him again."

Mary was looking intently at Troy, "You're going after Ace, arent you?" she asked quietly.

He wanted to tell her why he had to go. But it would only have frightened her. "Ace has to be curbed," he said. "Yesterday it was your dad. Last night it was Boone. No telling who it will be today."

Mary backed against one of the big pines. There was a strange light in her eyes as she looked at Troy. "I'm sorry I made you promise what you did last night, Troy," she said. "I know I was wrong. You've got to go after Ace."

"You won't hold it against me?"

She shook her head. "No. Aunt Lucy was right about you. She said you were a killer. Maybe it's not your fault; you were trained for it. It's what you've got to do.

"It looks that way," Troy said heavily, feeling a gulf widen between them.

"I'm sorry for everything that happened last night. I tried to tell myself that Aunt Lucy was wrong. You had killed twice but you wouldn't again; you weren't a killer. I thought that you and I—that we—" She broke off, biting her lip. "I was wrong. I was wrong to stop you from doing what you are destined to do."

Troy stepped towards her. "Does this make a difference—between us?"

She nodded. "You were born to kill, Troy. I see it now, and I won't stand in your way. But I can never love a killer. I'm sorry, Troy." There was something close to a sob in her voice as she turned and disappeared inside the cave.

Troy stared after her like one straining for a last glimpse of a fading paradise.

CHAPTER 16

IT SEEMED TO TROY THAT HE STOOD A LONG TIME facing down the canyon without moving to start on the mission he must accomplish.

He stirred finally, reaching for the reins on his roan. Waiting was not the answer. He had started to mount when he heard Dan call.

"What happened, Troy?" Dan asked, coming out of the cave. "Mary's crying."

"Nothing's happened," Troy said. "Mary hates killing, and it looks like there is some ahead."

Looking at his father, Troy knew that Dan was ready to ride again. But now Boone couldn't leave, and Troy had one more job to do before he'd be ready to go.

Dan came up to the roan's head. "What are you up to now?"

"Going hunting down in the valley."

"Something new pop up?"

"Ace Belling shot Boone last night. Boone's not hurt bad, but Belling's got to be stopped. Besides, I found out this morning exactly who was on that raid."

"Who?" Excitement quivered in Dan's voice.

"We got rid of four of them—the Swazeys, Emitt and Slagg. The other three are Jake Finley, Ace Belling, and King Purdy."

"Purdy?" The name exploded from Dan like a rifle shot.

"Do you know Purdy?" Troy asked, appalled by the hatred that twisted Dan's face.

Dan looked out over the canyon, his fingers curling into fists, then straightening. "I know the murdering skunk. And if I'd known he was here in this valley, I could have told you long ago he was the leader of that raid. Where does he live?"

"In town. He owns a saloon called the King's Palace. Where did you know him?"

"Back in Pennsylvania." Dan wheeled towards the cave. "Better get on with your hunting."

Troy watched his father disappear into the cave, then mounted and reined slowly into the trail. The expression he had seen on Dan's face when he had mentioned Purdy as one of the raiders stuck in his mind. Sometime in the past Dan and King Purdy had clashed. And hate still burned in Dan's heart.

Riding along the banks of Deer Creek, he considered

104

the situation. He knew the names of the raiders now, but somehow that fact in itself didn't seem so important any more. There were other things more pressing. Ace Belling stood out as the most dangerous element to be dealt with. Mary's safety hinged on Ace's elimination, not to mention his own safety and that of Boone and Kate. King Purdy, who had seemed to Troy a lesser figure, had suddenly taken on a more important role since Troy had seen Dan's reaction.

Jake Finley was a man whom Troy had known as well as anyone in the valley before the Willoubys left. Finley had made it a practice to drop in at the Willoubys every day or two for a short chat. There had been one unpleasant trait Troy had noted in the man. He was shifty and restless. Not a strong character, Troy decided.

Now Troy considered what faced him. His chance to help his marshal friend locate the stolen jewels had come, And he wouldn't have to deviate from his own battle. It was a good bet that the jewels were well concealed, and Ace and Purdy would never reveal their hiding place. Finley might be different. Troy had him pegged as the weak link of the three. He might be made to talk. It was worth a try, at least. Coming out in the valley, Troy reined at an angle towards the distant trail that would lead him to Jake Finley's ranch. He lifted the roan into a lope, and as he rode, he tried to piece together more of the puzzle, using the things he had learned from Barstow and later from Kate.

Barstow had said he had killed his man while stealing a box of jewels. It might just be possible that the jewels were the same ones Ace and Purdy had now. Ace had been the one who had been Barstow's partner in that deal. But Mike had said there had been nothing but paper and rocks in the box when they'd opened it. A

105

possible solution occurred to Troy. Ace was clever. Troy would be the last to deny that. It wasn't inconceivable that Ace had slipped the box away from Barstow and made the switch of rocks for jewels before Barstow and Ace had opened it together.

For a second Troy's reasoning bogged down as he wondered why three men with a box of priceless jewels would organize a gang and stoop to terror and murder just to acquire a little land and power. But that answer came quickly. The jewels were too hot to peddle. And they were as useless to the thieves as so many rocks from Storm Range. They needed money to carry them along till the jewels could be sold. Control of the valley was the answer. Dan Willouby had evidently been a stumbling-block to that power, so he had had to be eliminated. Emitt, Slagg, and the Swazeys had been taken on to do the necessary dirty work. But the real culprits were still at large in the valley.

Kate had said that only three of the gang knew about the jewels. And upon those three had been built the gang that had struck at the Willoubys. Troy remembered how his mother used to say it did no good to cut off the branches of a poisonous weed. It would grow again unless the evil roots were dug up. Then one of her favorite quotations came to his mind: "The love of money is the root of all evil."

Nearing Finley's ranch, Troy slowed his roan and sought an approach less conspicuous than the road. Half circling the place, he came into a ravine that angled past the barn and followed it until he was even with the old building. There he left his horse ground-hitched and ran the thirty yards to the rear of the barn.

He paused at the barn and listened. A hammer was pounding heavily on iron somewhere beyond the barn.

106

There must be a shop over there, Troy decided, and Finley was working in it. He had never been on the place before. In fact, he knew little about Finley except that he remembered he hadn't liked him too well. And he had been afraid of his wife, a big woman with stringy black hair that never seemed to be combed or pinned up and a temper that erupted like a volcano at the slightest excuse.

Checking his gun, Troy eased up the latch on the barn door. It swung back, and he found himself in a passageway that ran the length of the barn between two rows of stalls. The door at the far end of the barn opened into the yard. It was divided into two sections, with the top half open at the moment. Through the opening Troy could see the house.

Moving across the barn, he looked into the yard and located the shop where red-headed Jake Finley was working at an anvil. Even as he looked, Finley threw down his hammer and started towards the barn. Troy stepped back into the interior of the building. He hadn't expected to have it this easy.

But Finley didn't come into the barn. Troy heard his steps stop just outside and peered out cautiously over the bottom section of the door. Finley was stooped over a pile of old iron, sorting it over, mumbling to himself. Troy considered. When Finley found the piece of iron he wanted he would go back to his shop. And Troy would probably have a hard time getting the drop on him there. He glanced at the house. He admitted to himself that he would rather face Jake Finley on even terms than Mrs. Finley. If he stepped out here and got the drop on Jake, he would be in plain view of the house. But it was unlikely she would take a hand.

Lifting his gun, he kicked open the bottom half of the

door and stepped into the yard. Finley jerked upright with a surprised curse as lie heard the door creak.

"Easy does it, Jake," Troy said, showing the gun in his hand. "I just want to talk to you."

"Willouby!" Finley breathed. "What do you want?"

"A little information."

"I don't know anything," Finley said quickly, showing in his face that he thought his time had come.

"Maybe this gun will scrape a little of the rust off your memory. If you speak up, I'll give you a free ticket out of the valley like Swazey got."

"Why are you gunning for me? I ain't on your list."

"The list has been revised," Troy said. "Barstow and Hale have been taken off, and you and Ace Belling and Purdy are on it now."

The color faded from Finley's face. "Where did you find that out?" he croaked.

"Never mind where. I'm giving you a chance to get out with a whole skin. You can't hope for anything better."

"I didn't do any of the killing," Finley whined. "I swear I didn't. Ace and Purdy killed your folks."

"Forget about the raid," Troy said, his voice suddenly savage. "I want to know where those jewels are."

Finley's eyes widened. "What jewels?" he whispered in feigned surprise.

"You know what ones, Finley. You and Ace and Purdy have them. I want to know where they are. I'll give you till I count ten to start talking. They won't do you any good where you're going."

Finley licked his lips and swallowed hard. Indecision was in his eyes. Troy knew then that Finley had the answer he was seeking. But whether he would talk, even under the threat of his gun, was another matter.

108

Suddenly wild desperation came over Finley's face, and Troy knew he had lost. Finley's hand darted down to the gun tucked in his waistband. Troy had noticed it there and realized that Finley was keeping himself prepared for any emergency. And this was his emergency. He couldn't help knowing it was a futile effort. For Troy already had his gun in his hand.

But Finley couldn't know the battle going on inside Troy's mind. Troy didn't want to kill the red-headed rancher, at least not just yet. In Finley lay his only hope of learning the hiding place of the jewels. Neither Ace Belling nor Purdy would tell even under torture. Troy was sure of that. But with Finley it was different. In the next half-second he would have to kill Finley to save himself, and with Finley would go the secret he wanted to learn.

But there was one chance, Troy saw it and instantly took it. Having his gun in his hand gave him time enough to aim accurately, and he deliberately picked out Finley's leg and fired.

There was a loud snap when Troy's bullet hit, and Finley folded over as if he'd been clubbed. Troy saw the leg sticking out at an odd angle, and it struck him like a flash what he'd done. He had hit Finley's wooden leg and the leg had broken. But Finley wasn't hurt.

The red-headed rancher rolled over quickly, bringing up his gun. But Troy was standing over him by then, and he kicked the man's wrist. With a howl, Finley clutched his wrist, looking wildly towards his gun, which had clattered into the iron pile well out of his reach.

"Now then, talk," Troy demanded.

As he stepped back from Finley, something caught the sun and flashed in his eyes. He looked down and almost forgot the gun he was holding on Finley. From under Finley's pants leg one end of a sparkling necklace hung, dangling over the wooden stub of a leg.

The explanation struck Troy instantly. The hiding place for the jewels had been in Finley's wooden leg, which was hollow. The hollowness explained the ease with which the leg had broken at the impact of the bullet.

"Crawl back over there," Troy directed, nodding towards the open yard.

Finley obeyed sullenly. The necklace still dangled from his pants leg as he retreated, but a ring with a huge diamond set in a nest of smaller diamonds rolled out on the ground. Troy picked it up, then moved closer to Finley to pull the necklace free. These two would be all Finley would have. The marshal had told Troy there were two rings and two necklaces. One of the rings had been picked up in San Francisco, and Mary had the small necklace.

Troy heard the door of the house jerk open, and his head snapped up. Finley heard it, too, and tried to lunge up on his one good leg. Mrs. Finley was coming through the door, a cocked shotgun in her hands.

"Get out of the way, Jake," she screamed. "I'll get him."

Troy could have shot her before she could aim the scatter-gun, but it just wasn't in him to shoot a woman even in self-defence. Turning, he dived through the open barn door, sprawling in the loose hay on the floor. Behind him the shotgun roared, and he felt a sting as some of the pellets found their target. A loud cry in the yard whipped his glance back through the door as he leaped to his feet. Finley was on the ground again, and Troy saw that he was almost in line with the house. He

110

had intercepted a shot aimed at Troy.

Troy ran through the barn and across to the gully where his roan was waiting. He felt the pain where three or four pellets from the shotgun had lodged, and one in his hip was extremely aggravating, making him limp as he ran. As he mounted and wheeled his horse, he caught sight of Mrs. Finley just coming out the back door of the barn, brandishing the shotgun. Bending low over the saddle, Troy touched spurs to the roan and thundered down the gully out of range of Mrs. Finley's weapon.

CHAPTER 17

TROY CAME INTO TOWN BY WAY OF BACK ALLEYS. Now that Ace knew his secret was out, good sense prompted Troy not to show himself where Ace might get a sneak shot at him. Troy's fingers curled over his gun butt. If he could only meet Ace face to face! He had come here to do this chore, and it had already been put off too long.

Coming up to the back of the doctor's office, he dismounted, pushed open the rear door and went through the little room behind the office. Holmes looked up from his desk as Troy stepped into the office.

"What's wrong with the front door?" Holmes asked, rising.

"A trifle conspicuous," Troy said. "I'd like to get a little work done before I start looking for any more trouble."

"Carrying some lead?"

"Yeah." Troy nodded. "Buckshot."

"Who used a scatter-gun on you?"

"Mrs. Finley. Stop asking questions and get busy."

Holmes reached for his instruments as Troy started to undress. "So the old fire-eater backed up her words with buckshot. You should learn not to start trouble with her."

It didn't take the doctor long to dig out the shot. Troy was just ready to leave the office when guns opened up down the street. With the doctor, he raced for the door.

"Sounds like the Palace," Holmes said.

"Where does Kate live?" Troy asked, apprehension gripping him.

"Up this way." The doctor jerked a thumb in the opposite direction from the King's Palace. "It isn't Boone. He won't feel like starting anything like that for a few days."

Another shot rocked the still hot air; then the doors of the saloon slammed back and a man stumbled out and careened down the walk towards a horse tied in front of the barber shop just across from Holmes' office. Troy's blood went cold as he recognized his father.

Abandoning caution, Troy ran across the street towards Dan, expecting every instant to feel the searing rip of a bullet. But he reached Dan in the restless silence that followed the din of crashing guns. Without a word, Troy directed Dan's steps towards the doctor's office. Holmes met them in the street and took Dan's other arm.

In the office, they laid Dan on the cot Holmes kept there, and the doctor made a swift examination. At Troy's inquiring gaze, he shook his head. Dan, breathing hard, turned his eyes on Troy.

"Belling shot me," he said. "I was facing Purdy, ready to gun him down, when Belling shot me through a sliding panel in the bar. I ducked behind a table, but they were out of sight by then. The only way I could get

112

out was to make a break. They plugged me again when I tried."

The effort of talking sapped much of Dans remaining strength. After a moment, he looked at Holmes. "You can't pull me out of this, Doc."

"I'll try," Holmes said.

"You can't," Dan said with finality. "Troy, I've got something to tell you. I was hoping you'd never have to know, but you're on the trail now. You'll find out, anyway. I'd rather be the one to tell you."

Dan's breath was coming in ragged gasps and his voice was growing weaker as he talked. Troy glanced at Holmes and got his answer.

"You don't need to tell me anything, Dad," he said gently.

"I've got to. It's plagued me for years. You probably don't remember how hard up we were in Pennsylvania. It couldn't have been much worse. I gave up an honest living. I worked in a bank, and when the chance came to get away with some fancy jewels, I took it."

"Jewels?" Troy repeated in surprise.

"Yeah," Dan said. "The same ones you're so eager to get now. I found out when they were going to be taken from our bank and shipped out; I took the jewels and substituted rocks and paper. When it was found out that the jewels were gone, there was an awful stink. That's when we moved west. I settled in this valley, thinking I'd stay here till the fuss died down, then go on to the west coast and sell the stuff. Then Barstow came. I blamed him for our trouble. I didn't know Purdy was here."

Dan stopped, breathing hard. Troy watched him as if he were looking at a stranger.

"Where did you know Purdy?" he asked finally when

113

Dan was ready to talk again.

"Purdy was an outlaw back in Pennsylvania. I thought I'd outsmarted him in getting away with the jewels. But he must have trailed me somehow. Ace Belling is his right-hand man, and Ace crowded Barstow. They were after the jewels. I know now it must have been Purdy and Ace and Finley who broke into our back room the night of the raid and murdered Sarah and the kids. They got the jewels that night."

"But how could they know where you'd hidden them?" Troy still felt as if he were listening to a fairy tale.

"Finley pretended to be our friend and spent a lot of time at our place. He must have scouted around till he thought he knew where I kept them. Troy, they killed your mother, Ralph and Susie. It's up to you to settle that debt."

There was bitter hatred in Dan's voice; he began to cough as he finished speaking. Holmes leaned over him. When he stepped back, Dan looked up at Troy again, his breath coming in heavy gasps.

"I wish you'd let me handle Purdy myself," Troy said. "You weren't in any shape for a fight."

"I hated Purdy," Dan said between gasps. "He tried to get me to help him steal the jewels. I agreed, then double-crossed him to get the stuff for myself. I knew he'd try to catch me but I didn't think he could do it. The first I knew he was here was when you said so this morning." Sweat broke through Dan's skin as he labored to talk. "Kill him for me, Troy. Him and Ace Belling."

Misery twisted Dan's face, but still he struggled to talk. Now his words were barely coherent.

"Hale must have told Purdy. He was janitor in my bank. Followed me here. Blackmailed me. Must have told Purdy where I was." Dan's eyes were staring wildly at Troy and he tried to lift himself off the cot. "You've got to kill Purdy, Troy. Purdy and Belling. You've got to kill them. You've got to kill . . ."

He collapsed on the cot, the words dying in a mumble. Holmes dropped beside Dan, feeling for his pulse. But Troy knew the worst without waiting for the doctor's verdict. Still he waited till Holmes stood up, nodding silently. Then Troy turned slowly towards the door.

Outside, he paused. The sunlight was a mockery. It couldn't be a bright day. He. looked down at the King's Palace. Dan had stumbled out of there a few minutes before after trying to kill Purdy. At last he knew it was not a frightful nightmare. Dan was dead. But if there was any sorrow in Troy, it was smothered under the shock that dulled his senses.

For eight years, he had trained himself under Dan's guidance, preparing himself to be a knight of vengeance. But Dan hadn't come back to avenge his wife and children. He had come back for the jewels. And Troy had come to fight for him.

Troy moved aimlessly down the street. One question drummed over and over through his mind. How wrong could a man be and still think he was right? He had been wrong in condemning Mike Barstow. And the return of the Willoubys had brought destruction to the Barstow home and finally death to its head. He had come back to see that the crime committed against his father was righted. He had gone after the wrong man. Even Purdy and Belling were the wrong men. Dan Willouby was the right one. He had brought all the misfortune down on his own head by his original crime.

Justice! Troy walked faster, his teeth set tightly.

Willouby justice! There never had been such a thing. There never could be such a thing based on the foundation Dan Willouby had laid. King Purdy and Ace Belling deserved killing. Dan's last request had been for Troy to see that it was done. But there would be no more killing because Dan Willouby decreed it.

Troy's aimless march carried him past the King's Palace. His decision was made. He would ride back to the cave, get Mary and put her on the stage to go join her mother and brother, give her a clear title to the land she had called home and which was now his because Mike had given it to him. Then he would take the jewels to his marshal friend. And after that he would vanish from the earth as far as people he knew were concerned. He would reappear with a name free of the taint Dan had given the Willouby name and in a country where the past would never be revived.

His stride purposeful again, he turned towards the doctor's office to get his horse, which stood in the alley behind. But as he passed the Palace's doors this time, Kate ran out, catching his arm.

"Troy, you've got to do something."

Troy scowled. "I'm through doing things that are none of my business."

Kate's grip tightened. "This is your business. I know what's wrong with you. I was upstairs when your dad came into the Palace. I came down far enough to hear the whole thing."

"Then you ought to know why I'm through."

"You can't quit now. Not till Mary's safe."

A shock ran over him at the mention of Mary's name. "What's happened to Mary?"

"Nothing yet. But it soon will. She's at your cave, isn't she?"

116

Troy nodded. "Sure."

"Who's with her?"

Troy stopped for a second. With Dan dead and Boone here at Kate's shack, Mary was alone at the cave. "Nobody," he said, apprehension crawling through him.

"Then you'd better get there fast. Belling and Purdy are heading for the cave."

Troy felt sick. "Is Belling going after Mary?"

Kate shook her head. "He doesn't know she's there. But he won't hesitate to take her when he finds her."

"What is he going after?"

"The jewels."

Troy's hand went automatically to his pocket. "I've got them here."

"He thinks they're at the cave. Mrs. Finley rode in just after Ace shot your dad. She told what had happened out at the ranch. Finley's dead, and she said you got away with the jewels. Ace and Purdy were like madmen. They figured you'd go back to your hide-out, and they left as quick as they could get horses saddled."

"But they don't know where it is." Then a new fear struck him. Ace Belling had followed Barstow on the short cut and might know how to find the cave from there.

"They'll find it," Kate said positively. "They know it's somewhere up in Storm Range behind the big rock south of Barstow's. Ross Hale was in town with his dogs, and they hired him to find your trail. Those dogs will find the cave as sure as shooting."

"How much of a start do they have?"

"Only a few minutes. But that's plenty. You don't dare crowd them or they'll see you."

Troy started for the doctor's office. "Thanks, Kate. Take care of Boone."

117

"Boone will be all right. But you'd better watch your step."

With long strides, Troy hurried to his horse, mounted, and rode out on the street. Giving the roan his head, he lifted him into a lope, the thought of Mary's danger crowding everything else out of his mind.

CHAPTER 18

THE TOWN DROPPED BEHIND, AND TROY TURNED HIS gaze forward, searching for sign of the three riders. If he could come close enough to attract their attention, he could draw them into a chase and lead them away from the cave.

But he saw no sign of them except for the fresh tracks in the trail. He splashed across the ford, wishing Mary were in the big house instead of up in the cave.

South of the ford, he pushed the roan hard. If Ace knew where the cave was from the short cut, he would take that trail and there would be no way for Troy to beat him there. The best he could do then would be to overtake the three men if possible before they reached the cave, and to have it out. Ace didn't know that Mary was at the cave. If he knew that, Troy doubted if even the jewels would hold him back from her.

Troy was approaching the big rock when he first caught sight of them. Apparently they had ridden hard as far as the rock, knowing the trail to that point. But them they had trusted to the dogs. And now the dogs were leading them over the first knoll into the dry canyon that would eventually come out on the Deer Creek trail.

Troy knew a moment of relief when he saw the

direction they were going. The dogs were taking the long trail. But they were following it unerringly. It wouldn't take them long to get to the cave. Troy reined into the short cut. His hope lay in getting Mary away from the cave before they got there.

Troy put the roan into a climb, leaning far forward to make the going easier on the horse. There might be many more climbs like this before he and Mary were safe. For with the jewels hanging in the balance, Ace and Purdy would be persistent. And once they discovered Mary, the prize would be doubly inviting to Ace.

Once during the climb, Troy stopped the roan and dismounted. He chafed at the delay, but he had no choice. A horse, no matter how tough, could stand only so much. Then he was at the top and pushing down the narrow trail to the cave. Reaching it, he dismounted and paused a moment, listening. There was no sound from the lower trail. But somewhere down there two dogs were silently and swiftly leading three men up the trail, men with murder and greed in their hearts.

Ground-hitching his heaving roan, Troy ran into the cave. Mary met him just inside the entrance, her face showing the worry and fear that gripped her.

"Where's your dad, Troy?" she asked before he could say a word. "He left here just after you did."

"He went after Purdy. Ace killed him. We've got to get away from here. I'll catch your horse. Bring your saddle."

"What's wrong, Troy?" Panic forced her voice to a shrill pitch.

"Ace is coming here. Purdy and Hale are with him."

He didn't stop to explain further. Every second counted now. Those dogs would follow the trail as fast as the men could ride. They would be coming up the canyon trail to the cave in a few minutes.

Troy sent his gaze over the slope above the cave. And he instantly discarded any idea of trying to make a stand at the cave. It would be an easy matter to crawl up the slope and come down above the cave entrance. Anyway, it was too dangerous for Mary. She might be hit in a fight. Or even worse, he might be the one to fall, leaving her to Ace. His only chance lay in running. Once he got her to safety, he could come back and give Ace and Purdy all the fight they wanted.

Mary's black horse kept just out of Troy's reach as he ran up the slope to catch it. Silently he cursed it for the precious seconds it was making them lose. Mary could have caught it, he knew, but the horse wasn't taking kindly to his abrupt approach. With an effort he slowed to an easy walk, reaching out coaxingly for the horse's mane.

Minutes passed; they seemed like hours to Troy. The horse, excited now, continued to elude his reaching fingers. Nerves strained to breaking point, he imagined he heard the bay of a hound down the canyon.

He tried to find another solution. But there was no other horse here. And it would be suicide to start out riding the roan double. The black had to be caught. In desperation, he lunged at the horse. The black reared back, but it was too late to escape Troy's surprise attack. Troy got a hand locked in the mane and hung on. Realizing it was caught, the horse subsided docilely and followed Troy down the slope to the front of the cave.

But precious minutes had been lost. Mary had the saddle waiting. As Troy slapped the saddle on and pulled the cinch tight, she brought the bridle.

"Are we leaving for good?" she asked.

120

"Probably. But don't bring a thing that will weigh down your horse. Ride easy and keep him as fresh as you can."

"Do you think they're close?"

Troy held the black while she mounted. "Too close. They're using Hale's dogs, so we'll have a tough time shaking them."

"Where are we going, Troy?"

"Queen City. I want to get you on the stage out of this country."

Troy put his roan to the ascent, and Mary's horse fell in behind, heading up the look-out trail. It was the only trail out from the cave that wouldn't bring them face to face with Ace and Purdy.

"We're going in the wrong direction for Queen City," Mary reminded him when Troy reined up to listen and look down their back trail.

Troy nodded. "In this case, the longest way around might be the shortest and surest way."

"Are we going through the valley?"

Troy shook his head as he urged his horse forward. "They'd see us from the look-out before we got out of sight. Once they got us spotted, we'd never be able to dodge them. We'll circle back through the hills."

Only the creak of saddle leather and the labored breathing of the horses broke the silence as they neared the look-out. Then suddenly the eager throaty bay of a hound ripped through the stillness. Troy wheeled in the saddle to look back and met Mary's frightened gaze.

"They're not very far away," Mary said in a tight whisper.

"At the cave," Troy said grimly. "They've found the fresh scent. They'll come fast now."

"What will we do, Troy? We can't outrun the

121

hounds."

"Ace and Purdy aren't riding hounds," Troy said briefly. "Keep riding. We'll stay ahead as long as we can."

After their first excited bay, the hounds subsided. Troy was thankful for that. Their baying made his spine prickle. But by the time he and Mary reached the lookout, he was wishing the hounds would sound off again. The menacing silence behind him was more nerveracking than the bloodthirsty yelps of the dogs. They were close. They were bound to be, for they would travel much faster than horses. But Troy could only guess how close.

They cut across the little level spot overlooking the valley, and Troy led the way through scattered boulders and trees along the edge of the wall that rose abruptly from the floor of Storm Valley. Then the ground dipped sharply and trees closed in around them.

Troy aimed at a spot on top of the ridge across the little valley, only vaguely remembering this country from his boyhood explorations. About five miles from the cave, he recalled, was a big valley that cut through the range and led out to the stage road to Queen City. If they could shake their pursuers before they got to that valley, they should be able to get to Queen City safely.

An occasional excited yelp came from the dogs now as their trail got warmer. Each outburst placed the hounds closer to their quarry. At the bottom of the little canyon, Troy called a halt to let their horses blow.

"We can't keep ahead of them much farther," Mary said, despair in her voice.

"I know." Troy nodded. "We won't try it much farther."

They pushed up the slope, finally turning into a dim

deer trail. It ran straight for a hundred yards, angling up the hillside, and Troy followed it. When it turned to run parallel with the top of the ridge, Troy pulled off and stopped. Dismounting, he handed his reins to Mary.

"Why are we stopping?" Mary asked excitedly. "We can't afford to lose any time."

"This won't be time lost," Troy said grimly, sliding the rifle out of his saddle boot.

"But if you shoot the dogs, it will tell Ace and Purdy where we are."

"Those hounds are doing that with every yelp. You can bet Hale can tell from the sound of their yelping how hot the trail is."

Troy moved over until he had a clear view down the straight trail. Pumping a shell into the chamber of his rifle, he knelt on one knee and waited. From across the canyon came the sound of horses crashing through the underbrush.

"They're not far behind," Mary said softly, her voice revealing her terror.

"They won't get any farther behind as long as those dogs keep on our trail."

It seemed an eternity to Troy, although he knew it had really been less than a minute, before he heard a sharp yelp just below the spot where his vision ended.

Then the first hound broke into the dim trail, his ugly head bent low, nose to the ground, ears flopping as he loped along. The other dog was only two lengths behind. Lifting his rifle, Troy took careful aim and squeezed the trigger. The lead hound collapsed, turning a double somersault before sliding to a quivering stop, stretched full length across the trail.

The other hound halted abruptly, his head jerking up. At sight of Troy crouched in the trail, he curled back his lips in a vicious snarl and leaped forward, clearing his fallen companion and bearing down on Troy.

Troy quickly pumped another shell into his rifle and calmly took aim. His shot stopped the hound only ten yards away. As the echo of the shot died, a yell came up from the bottom of the little canyon. Troy wheeled to his horse and jammed the rifle back in its boot.

"Hale has guessed what's happened," he said as he mounted. "He'd shoot a man quicker for hurting one of his dogs than he would for trying to kill him."

Troy led the way up the slope, crowding the horses. Now was the time to put distance between them and Purdy's men. For once Troy and Mary were out of earshot and without the dogs on their trail, it shouldn't be hard to lose them in this rough country.

Threading his way through the pines and spruce. Troy angled a little north of west. Mary kept close behind him. Occasionally he paused. He could invariably hear the pursuit. But each time it seemed to be farther away.

Then he struck a rough rocky area. Cautioning Mary to follow closely and not to let her horse step in any soft dirt among the rocks, he moved ahead, steering his course more to the north-west.

"Isn't this a good place to turn towards Queen City?" Mary asked, glancing nervously behind. "They'd miss our trail here."

Troy shook his head. "That's what they'll expect us to do. While they're over on the south edge of this rock pile looking for our tracks, we'll be putting miles between us and this place. Then when they find out where we did go, we'll be so far ahead, it won't make any difference."

Troy tried to make it sound convincing. But he knew a tracker like Hale wouldn't lose much time locating the spot where they had left the rocks. He only hoped it would take Hale long enough to allow Mary and him to make it over the next two ridges into the valley leading down to Queen City. From there they would depend on the speed of their horses.

After leaving the rocks, Troy didn't stop until they reached the top of the next ridge. There he paused and listened intently for a minute. But there was no sound behind. Either the pursuers were still stranded on the rocks looking for the trail or they had actually been thrown off the track. Troy wanted to believe the latter but couldn't. They were coming and they would keep on coming until they caught him or he had Mary safe in Queen City.

He looked back at Mary. Worry was in her face, and with it a nervous tension that drove out all other emotions.

Before dropping down into the big valley running towards Queen City, he paused and listened long and carefully. There was no sound behind. But he refused to let himself be taken off guard. Ace and Purdy were not ones to give up this easily, especially when the prize was so great.

They dropped down off the ridge. Pointing towards Queen City, they slackened the reins and let the horses choose the pace, a ground-eating lope.

The first inkling of danger came with the riders that plunged into the trail ahead. He saw all three almost at once—Ace and Purdy in the lead, Hale in the background. Fleetingly he wondered how they had gotten ahead.

Then his hand dived for his gun. But he knew he had no chance. Ace had his gun in his hand as his horse plunged into the trail. There was a mocking grin on

125

Ace's face now. His gun was centered, and Troy tried to dodge but realized he couldn't. Ace was too close and too sure a shot. His own gun was half out of leather when the world exploded and he felt himself falling. . . .

CHAPTER 19

IT WAS A NIGHTMARE TO MARY. SHE SAW THE THREE horses burst out of the trees, and paralysis gripped her. She knew Troy was trying to reach his gun, and Ace's diabolical grin was enough to tell her that he had no chance. When she tried to scream, no sound came. Then Ace's gun roared and Troy jerked back in the saddle, his gun slipping from his hand, sagging and finally sliding back into the holster. For a horrible moment, Troy balanced in the saddle before he lurched sideways off his roan. Ace nudged his horse forward, gun ready, watching Troy. It was then Mary regained control of her muscles. She kicked her black towards Ace.

"You murderer!" she screamed, and threw herself off her horse to run to Troy.

But Ace was on the ground as soon as she was. He grabbed her arm and gripped it like a vice. "Take it easy, Mary. There ain't no use fretting over him now. I don't miss a shot as close as that. If you want to make a fuss over somebody, make it over me."

He laughed as she tried to squirm out of his grasp, his fingers biting into her flesh like steel bands. Purdy pushed his horse up to them.

"Are you going to get those jewels, Ace, or am I going to have to get off and do it?"

Ace looked up at Purdy. "Be quite a job for you to get off that horse, wouldn't it? I'll get them. Don't get in a

126

sweat. I'm just luckier than you. I win twice on this deal."

Ace released Mary then and stepped towards Troy. Mary backed towards her horse, reaching for the reins. There was nothing she could do for Troy. The bullet had struck him in the head, and blood already covered one side of his face. He lay as he had fallen without so much as moving a finger. The only thing left for her now was to get away. She had always hated and feared Ace Belling. Her father had feared him and had died because he defied him. Now Troy had fallen before Ace's gun trying to protect her.

No one was watching her. Ace had found the pocket in Troy's shirt where the jewels were concealed and had brought them out into the late sun, which hung only half an hour above the western rim of the valley. Purdy was leaning from his saddle, looking at the sparkling diamonds, and Hale had crowded close, his eyes bulging.

Mary reached the reins, gathered them up, and turned to her horse. She had one foot in the stirrup when Ace looked up.

"Stop her," Ace yelled, leaping to his feet.

"Let her go," Purdy said without interest.

But Ace lunged for his horse. Mary was in the saddle and wheeling her black. She noted that Hale was standing back, watching passively. It was all up to Ace.

Digging in her heels, she headed the black towards the upper end of the valley where the traveling looked easier. Direction meant little right now. She heard Ace behind her, riding hard, hurling a curse back at his companions for not joining in the chase.

Mary gave the black his head. The horse seemed to understand the urgency driving his mistress and stretched out his legs. Mary bent low over the saddle, talking in the black's ear, urging him to greater effort.

Glancing back, she saw that she wasn't gaining on Ace. Ace's mount was a rangy white horse, and Mary realized that only a miracle would allow her black to outdistance him. Still she urged him on, and for another hundred yards the distance separating them didn't change.

Then slowly the white horse began to gain a yard, then five. Mary knew the miracle wasn't going to happen. Ace's big white horse inched closer until he was a mere ten feet behind the black. Then suddenly Mary pulled in on the reins and wheeled her black. Ace shot past before he could come to a halt. By the time he had turned, Mary had a twenty-yard lead again.

But she knew that couldn't last. The black had been ridden hard, and it was too much to ask him to perform the impossible. This time as Ace pulled in behind her, he rode more cautiously, ready to make a sudden turn. But Mary didn't turn. There was no use.

Ace came alongside, reached over and grabbed the black's reins. Mary pulled up before Ace had a chance to jerk the black down.

Ace grinned. "Looks like you're going to take a little taming."

Mary kept a rigid silence as Ace led the way back to Purdy and Hale.

"Where's that other necklace?" Purdy demanded as Ace stopped, still holding the black's reins.

"Mary's got it," Ace said easily. "That means I've got it now."

"Just be sure," Purdy said. "Come on. Let's find a place to camp. We can't get back to town tonight."

They moved up the valley, Purdy leading the way

now. He slopped over the saddle like a bulging sack of grain. But Mary gave little thought to Purdy, or even to Ace. Her mind stayed on Troy as she had seen him last, still and lifeless. It could all be laid at her door. She had held Troy back when he had wanted to go after Ace. Boone wouldn't be laid up with wounds now if Troy had killed Ace right after Ace had shot Mike. And Dan Willouby might still be alive. And now because of her, because he had tried to get her out to safety, Troy had gone down before Ace's gun.

If she could only go back to Troy! There was just the slimmest chance that Troy was still alive. But to that dim hope she clung. There was no other hope now.

Purdy twisted in the saddle finally and motioned to Hale. Hale kicked his horse up even with the big man.

"Pick out a camp site, Hale. You know this country, don't you?"

"Sure," Hale said in his sharp shrill voice. "I know every foot of these hills. How else do you think I figured out where Willouby would be likely to go when we lost his trail?"

"Never mind that," Purdy said irritably. "Just find us a place to camp."

Hale squinted through the gathering dusk and finally rode off to one side. When he came back, he motioned for the others to follow him. The hermit led the way up a hill to a spot well protected from the chilly breeze by a thick stand of pines.

"You won't find a better place to camp in ten miles," Hale said proudly. "Good shelter here. And there's a spring about fifty yards down the hill."

"Stop babbling and get some supper," Purdy ordered. "I'm starved."

Hale scowled at the big man and squirted tobacco

129

juice through his snaggle teeth. "I hired out as a guide and tracker, not a camp cook. I'll help get supper, but I ain't going to do it all."

"Don't get your back up," Ace said as he slid off his horse. "As soon as I hobble this little filly, I'll help you even if King won't."

Ace came towards Mary's horse as if to lift her out of the saddle, but she stepped down before he got there. He grinned and reached for her arm, grabbing it before she could jerk away.

"No use acting shy," he said easily. "You promised to be my girl once. Remember? This time youre not going to get the chance to back out. Tomorrow we're getting the justice of the peace to marry us right here in Big Pine."

A shiver traveled down her spine, but she nodded. Maybe if she pretended to submit to his wishes his guard would relax a little, just enough for her to make another break. And the next one had to be successful.

"That's showing good sense," Ace said triumphantly. "No use kicking over the traces when your luck has run out."

He took his rope from the saddle horn and came towards Mary, uncoiling it. She gasped as she realized his intentions.

"You wouldn't tie me like an outlaw, would you?" she demanded, despair in her voice.

"I don't like to, Mary. But I said you wasn't getting the chance to back out again. I can't stay awake all night to watch you, so I've got to fix it so you won't need watching. I won't pull the rope too tight."

True to his word, Ace didn't pull the ropes tight enough to bite into her wrists or ankles, but they were tied in hard knots that she couldn't untie. The long end of the rope was tied to a tree, and Mary found herself helpless. A cold sick fear grew in her.

Her hands were released to let her eat supper, but her appetite was gone. Ace was almost apologetic when he came to tie her again.

"I wouldn't use nothing but hobbles on you, but you'd untie them if I didn't keep your hands out of mischief. I'll make a bed for you here. You'll be comfortable."

Ace brought blankets and made her a bed, then took his own bedroll over by the fire and unrolled it. Hale brought his own roll up close to Mary and flipped it open.

"Don't mind if I sleep here, do you?" he asked. "Figured I'd like it here." He scowled at the two men crawling into their blankets by the dying fire. "I don't take kindly to the idea of tying up women."

A wave of gratitude swept over Mazy as she looked at the dirty, ragged man. He lived on money he extorted as his price for keeping or telling the secrets he knew, but he had some scruples at least.

Mary tried to make herself comfortable under her blankets and almost succeeded. But her thoughts would not let her rest. Each time she closed her eyes, she saw Troy slumping off his horse, to lie still and limp. Again and again there hammered through her mind the thought that she was to blame. If she had approved instead of opposing him when he had first wanted to go after Ace, this might not have happened.

She turned in her blankets, the ropes hampering the movement. Always she saw Troy falling from his horse, and the words, "too late," beat through her mind like a chant. There was no sleep for her, and the night wore on into an endless eternity.

Dawn finally came, and Mary watched with wide sleepless eyes as it spread across the sky. Every muscle seemed to ache from contact with the hard ground.

Hale stirred first, crawling out of his blankets and rolling them up. He started the fire, and Ace and Purdy came to life. Nothing was said, not even a morning greeting, until Hale had the coffee pot over the blaze. Then the hermit broke the silence.

"You can get along now without me, I reckon."

Ace stretched and yawned. "Sure. We don't need you any more."

"How about my pay?"

"Fifty bucks. I'll pay you after breakfast."

"Two hundred and fifty," Hale said sharply. "Those dogs were worth a hundred apiece."

"I didn't kill your dogs. Take it out of Willouby's carcass."

Hale advanced threateningly on Ace. "They were helping trail down Willouby for you. You'll pay me for them."

"Don't be too sure about it, Hale," Purdy warned. "We don't need you any more, you know."

Hale stood his ground. "I just want what I've earned. I did my job."

"You didn't earn anything," Ace said lazily.

"Why, you polecat!" Hale took two giant strides towards the little gambler, then stopped short, looking into the bore of Ace's gun.

"This is what you've earned, Hale," Ace said softly. "If you insist, you'll get it. Otherwise, you'd better start towards the valley. Don't bother to take your horse. Walking's not crowded."

For a second Hale stood facing the gambler, and Mary held her breath, certain the hermit was going to rush in to meet certain death. Then slowly he turned and walked into the trees to the north, not looking back.

Ace watched him till he disappeared, then let his gun slide back into his holster. With a grin, he moved across to Mary.

"Looks like a lucky day for me," he said. "A dollar saved is a dollar earned. Now don't go away. I'll be back."

He grinned at Mary's frown. She didn't want to give him the pleasure of seeing her discomfort, but she couldn't help herself. Ace got a big dipper and disappeared down the slope in the direction of the spring. Mary leaned against the tree, her spirits at a low ebb.

CHAPTER 20

WHEN THE FIRST GLIMMER OF CONSCIOUSNESS FORCED Troy's eyes open, it was dark. His only sensation for the moment was a hammering headache. He closed his eyes again against the pain. His hand went to his head and came away sticky with half-dried blood. He wanted to sink back into painless oblivion.

Then slowly things began to loom up out of the haze. He remembered the chase when Ace and Purdy and Hale had tried to catch him. Then they had suddenly appeared directly in front of him. Ace had had a gun in his hand. Troy had tried to reach his.

Then Mary burst into his thoughts. He tried to sit up, but dropped back as pain flashed through his head. In a minute he tried again, struggling to a sitting position. Ace must have Mary now. The thought possessed him, held him erect till the night around him stopped spinning.

He staggered to his feet, one hand pressed tightly to his head, trying to suppress the pain. His thinking was still fuzzy, but he remembered that a little stream ran through the valley and he aimed his uncertain steps in the direction in which he thought it lay.

Coming to a tree, he paused, his head throbbing until it seemed he couldn't go on. Then he remembered the jewels and felt in his pocket for them. He hadn't had time since taking them from Finley to put them in any safe carrying place. Now they were gone. The jewels more than Mary had been the motive behind Ace's attack. But Ace wouldn't hesitate to take his double prize.

He staggered on and finally heard the ripple of water. Reaching the stream, he knelt beside it. Only when his gun tipped forward on his hip was he conscious of it. Surprise prompted him to lift it from the holster and examine it. He hadn't expected Belling to leave his gun even if he had been certain Troy was dead. But there had been the jewels and Mary to think of. Ace's neglect could be overlooked.

Satisfied that the gun was in perfect order and loaded, he laid it beside him and dipped a hand into the cold water. He splashed the water over his face and head, the chill of it dulling the pain momentarily.

It might have been an hour, maybe two or three, that he stayed beside the stream after washing the wound as best he could. He didn't need a doctor to tell him that he had escaped death by a mere fraction of an inch.

When the first dim streaks of dawn came up out of the east, he left the stream. He was surprised that his steps were steady. Aside from a dull throbbing headache and a dragging weariness, he felt ready for the task ahead of him.

At the scene of the attack, he found the trail. His horse was nowhere in sight, but that didn't stop him. He would follow the trail on foot if he had to. How far or how long it would be, he had no idea. But he would follow till he dropped.

The light was strong enough for him to locate his hat, and he put it on gingerly. It would have to serve as a bandage for his wound.

The sun was almost up when he stopped suddenly, lifting his nose into the light breeze. Wood smoke was drifting to him. A grim satisfaction coursed through Troy. The trail was much warmer than he had expected.

Forgetting the tracks he had been following, he moved ahead, directly into the wind. He found himself climbing a hill; the odor of burning pine was getting stronger by the minute. Then he was at the top of the knoll, and ahead of him was the fire. He saw Mary first, sitting beside a tree several feet from the fire. On the opposite side, coming up with more wood, was King Purdy. Ace Belling was nowhere in sight.

Tension drove the weariness out of Troy's muscles, but not even the impending crisis could dissipate the ache in his head. He lifted his gun, and it felt unusually heavy in his hand. Keeping the trees between him and Purdy, he moved forward, searching the area around the camp for Belling. But the little gambler was nowhere to be seen. It sent an uneasy tremor over Troy, and he stopped out of sight of the camp. Ace would surely put in an appearance soon.

Purdy moved around the fire, finally pouring a cup of coffee and moving towards Mary with it. Setting it on the ground, he untied her hands, then handed the cup to her.

"Ain't no sense waiting for Ace," Purdy said. "You'll have plenty of mornings to serve breakfast to him. Drink some coffee, and we'll have the rest pretty soon."

Purdy's words stung Troy like the lash of a whip. Before he realized it, he was in the circle of the camp, his gun trained on Purdy. Mary dropped her cup, spilling the coffee, but her startled gasp was all but lost on Troy. His eyes were fastened on Purdy's face, which had turned a pasty gray at sight of him.

"Willouby!" Purdy breathed as if he were looking at a ghost. "Ace killed you," he added foolishly.

"Not dead enough," Troy snapped. "Maybe you can do a better job."

Composure began coming back to the big man. With an effort, he steadied his voice. "I'm not crazy enough to draw against a cocked gun."

Almost involuntarily Troy found himself lowering his gun towards his holster. He knew the risk and he knew the treachery that was at Purdy's command. But no matter what else Dan Willouby had done, he had taught his boys to be square-shooters. Troy couldn't break that habit now. His gun settled into leather.

"Don't, Troy," Mary screamed as if just finding her voice.

But Troy watched Purdy. Mary's screams seemed to be a signal to the big man. His hand dropped with the swiftness of an eagle's dive. But it wasn't fast enough. The weariness was gone from Troy's arm as he whipped up his gun and fired a split-second ahead of the big saloon keeper. Purdy's jaw dropped and he backed a step as if hit with a club. His .45 blazed once, the bullet ploughing into the ground; then the gun dropped a foot in front of Mary. He backed another step or two before collapsing.

Troy turned to Mary, expecting to see in her eyes a horror that would turn to revulsion the second she looked at him. But she wasn't looking at either Purdy or him. Her eyes were fixed on something behind him, and the look on her face sent a chill racing up his spine.

Before he could spin around, she jerked forward, reaching for Purdy's gun. The gun was within her reach, and she whipped it up, squeezing the trigger.

Troy was whirling as she moved, and saw Ace Belling at the edge of the little clearing where the camp had been made. His gun was in his hand and he was bearing down on Troy's back. Mary's shot was wild, but it startled the gambler, and for a split second he jerked back, his aim destroyed. Then he came to himself and relined his sights.

But now Troy was in the fight. His shot joined the thunder of Ace's gun. Troy's left leg was jerked from under him and he went down on his face. He rolled over, bringing up his gun, expecting the burn of another bullet as Ace leaped in for the kill. But there was no bullet, and for a second the world spun before Troy's eyes so that he couldn't locate Ace. Then he saw him lifting himself to his knees, his gun pointing unsteadily towards Troy. Troy's gun focused and roared again. Ace folded like a punctured balloon.

It was over then, and an unbearable weariness descended on Troy. He dropped back on the ground, fighting the blackness creeping in on him and knowing it was a losing battle.

He was aware first of Mary brushing the dust from his face. When he tried to sit up, she pushed him back gently.

"You've had enough for a while, Troy," she said softly. "Just be quiet. I'll get some water from the

137

spring."

Troy remembered then. Purdy and Ace. And here was Mary working over him with a gentleness he had never expected to experience. And she was no longer shackled with ropes. "I thought you were tied to that tree," he said.

"Purdy took the ropes off my hands for breakfast. I untied the other knots."

Then he remembered her wild lunge for Purdy's gun and the shot she had sent in Ace's direction that had meant the difference between life and death for him. He struggled to a sitting position as the marvel of it struck him. She, who held the power to keep him back from a killer's trail and had used that power more than once, had actually sided him when the chips were down. Purdy's gun still lay but a few feet away. He nodded towards it. "You might have hurt somebody with that gun."

Her face was sober, her eyes wide and thoughtful. "I know. I might have killed Ace. I just couldn't shoot straight enough."

"You mean you aimed at him?" Troy said, unbelieving.

She nodded. "The best I could." Her head bowed. "I've been wrong, Troy. I couldn't see that all this had to be and that you had to have a part in it. I held you back. This might not have happened if it hadn't been for me."

A hope, exciting in its promise, was bubbling up in Troy. "If it hadn't happened this way, it would have happened some other way," he said. "It had to come."

"But Boone might not have been hurt. And your dad. And last night I was sure Ace had killed you. It was my fault." Tears filmed her eyes.

"That shot you took at Ace more than paid for every mistake you think you've made. That saved my life." Looking at her, he suddenly had to ask one question. "You said once you couldn't love a killer. Does that still stand?"

She nodded, not looking up. "I always thought of a killer as a man who went out looking for gunfights. People said you were a killer, and some thought you had come to terrorize Storm Valley. I know now you fought only when you had to, and you were fighting for an ideal. I could love a man like that."

Her voice was so low that Troy barely caught her words. The hope that had come to life in him surged up triumphantly. He reached out, pulling her to him. She came willingly, lifting her lips for his kiss.

He knew at that moment that it had all been worth it. The guns at last were still, and in their place would come the peace and love for which every man lives and hopes.

We hope that you enjoyed reading this
Sagebrush Large Print Western.
If you would like to read more Sagebrush titles,
ask your librarian or contact the Publishers:

United States and Canada

Thomas T. Beeler, *Publisher*
Post Office Box 659
Hampton Falls, New Hampshire 03844-0659
(800) 251-8726

United Kingdom, Eire, and
the Republic of South Africa

Isis Publishing Ltd
7 Centremead
Osney Mead
Oxford OX2 0ES England
(01865) 250333

Australia and New Zealand

Australian Large Print Audio & Video P/L
17 Mohr Street
Tullamarine, Victoria, 3043, Australia
1 800 335 364